ROSE MOXHAM was born in Camden and lives in Sydney. She writes and teaches fiction at the University of Technology, Sydney. *Teeth Marks* is her second novel. What she likes best is reading and writing and travelling. Rose is currently in Hanoi in Vietnam where she is working with translators on an anthology of a thousand years of Vietnamese poetry.

TEETH MARKS

ROSE MOXHAM

First published in 2007

Allen & Unwin
83 Alexander St
Crows Nest NSW 2065
Australia
Phone: (61 2) 8425 0100
Fax: (61 2) 9906 2218
Email: info@allenandunwin.com
Web: www.allenandunwin.com

National Library of Australia
Cataloguing-in-Publication entry:
Moxham, Rose, 1953–.
Teeth marks.

For young adults.
ISBN 978 1 74114 771 1 (pbk.).

I. Title

Cover photograph by James Pauls/iStockphoto
Text and Cover Design by Mathematics www.xy-1.com
Set in 11/16.5pt Bembo by Midland Typesetters, Australia
Printed in Australia by McPherson's Printing Group

10 9 8 7 6 5 4 3 2 1

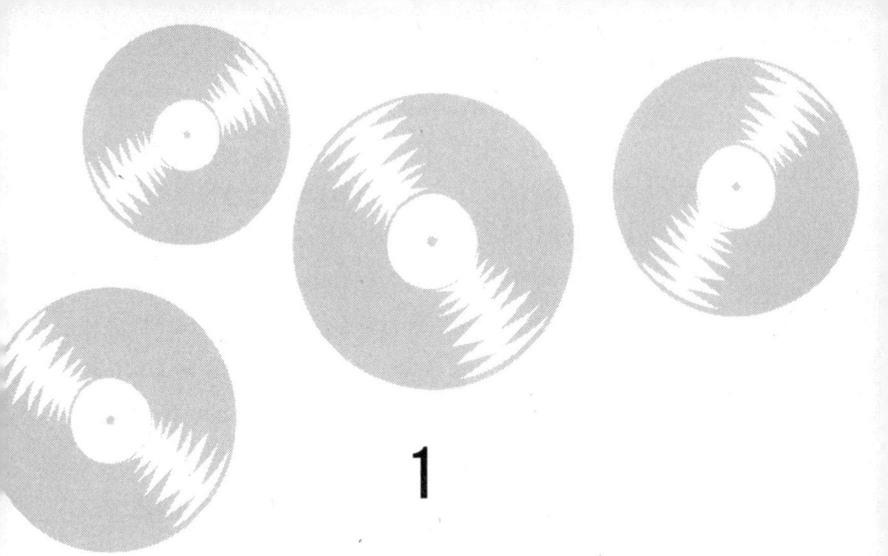

1

NICK STOOD OUTSIDE THE PUB UNTIL THE SALOON DOORS stopped swinging. His helmet felt heavy, as if all the night's bitterness had been scooped into it. It was just another thing to crush his pride. He slipped the chinstrap over the handlebar and mounted the bicycle.

The doors flapped again as Robbie emerged with his arm slung around the Irish girl. 'Back to the bad old days, mate!' he yelled gleefully as Nick took off down the hill.

The wind felt perilous. It numbed his ears and pinned his mouth back into a crazy grin. All this speed – it felt good. He didn't bother with the brakes, gave up trying to get a grip on the pedals. He spread his legs and let the steep incline carry him, hurtling past those stagnant shops, past the sleeping homeless guy, overtaking a car. The dogs free, barking and running after him. They loved him, even if Jude didn't. And at the bottom of the hill, coming up to meet him like two pearly torpedoes, were Dave Bear-claw's spectacularly white winkle-picking shoes. He'd done what Robbie had told him and spruced up his feet. Dave Bear-claw stepped out onto the road to wave at Max turning the corner in his beat-up ute.

The dogs were howling down the hill and so was Nick, who swerved to save Dave's shoes at the very instant that Dave stepped back. As Nick lost control of the bike he heard the dogs barking joyfully at Max as if he were the prodigal son home at last. Fear made Nick fling out his hands to protect his face, to save it from ending up like his heart. His head had to take care of itself. Nick sailed past the flash of Dave Bear-claw's ringed fingers, still raised in greeting to Max – or raised in thanks to some god for not letting him be run down by a fool on a bicycle. Or raised to say 'Stop!'

Too late, Nick was on his way.

2

THIS IS WHAT HAPPENS.

Strangers come, flashing a torch into his face every hour, demanding that he tells them what day it is and what his name is. They pinch his toes and his fingers to make sure they're still attached and that he has a grip on all the different kinds of pain. They take away his clothes, wrap him in plaster, drape him in a gown and deposit him on a trolley. He lies there waiting for someone to give him a drink, and then he waits for them to bring him a bottle so he can piss it out. A nurse brings a blue plastic thing shaped like a teardrop and plonks his dick into it. *How can you piss into that?* At last he does, and then he waits for somebody to take it away. While he waits he wonders whether it was really Jude's face hovering over him in the ambulance, or another delusion. He forgets the bottle is still there.

He reads Nurse Sunni's nametag and hears her practiced little sigh as she mops up the urine from his plaster and washes him down none too gently. She rolls him over to get the sheet out from under him, and back again to insert a clean one. Every roll and flick of the sheet hurts, but Nurse Sunni is right because *it gets the blood moving and you'll be less prone to bedsores, Mr Green.* With thin eyes and a tight smile she snaps the sheet over him.

In the small hours they move him into a ward. His arms have been cemented all the way, past his wrists, so he can't even move his fingers. Each end of the pin poking through the knee of his right leg is attached to strings and pulleys that go to the end of the bed and over it, where a weight hangs, keeping his leg nice and straight. Only his left leg is free. He could tap five toes if music hadn't abandoned him. The only beat is his pulse and that's getting feathery.

There's a voice behind his eyes saying he could have done things differently. But he doesn't know what, or how, and after all, it's only a voice.

When Nick woke there was a strand of hair in his mouth that he couldn't spit out, and an old man was glaring at him from the next bed. At the foot of his bed was a woman who was roughly the size and shape of a thunderhead. For a moment his pain shrank in her presence. Moonfaced, heavy eyes outlined in black like Cleopatra, she wore a pink cotton blouse with a burst seam across one lumpy shoulder. A boxy black purse hung from the other. She was holding his patient-chart and her absurdly soft and breathy voice wafted over him, giving him news of himself.

'His name's Nick Green and he's fractured. They'd ship him home,' she said, pausing to give him a slow wink, 'but nobody's there, so he's in for a few weeks.'

'Sounds like a drifter, and a bloody noisy one.' The old man's red-eyed stare reminded Nick of a cattle prod. 'Kept me awake with your howls, you did.'

'Well, he's all broken up,' the giant woman said. 'He's got plenty to howl about.' She read more from the chart. 'Bilateral compound fractures of the radius, ulna and carpus bones.' She nodded at the plaster encasing Nick's forearms and wrists. 'And mid-compound fracture of the right femur. That'll be your leg,' she informed him with a cheery smile. 'Broken the same as Al's was.' She turned to the old man. 'You remember that, Eric? When Al slipped over last year?'

Eric nodded. 'A disgrace.'

'Al's from my ward,' the woman burbled at Nick, pointing to a vacant-faced man in the bed opposite his. 'Say hullo to Nick, Al.' Al waved feebly as the woman replaced Nick's chart at the end of his bed. 'He broke it when he slipped on his tapioca pudding.' She advanced towards Nick, her short purple skirt straining helplessly against her thighs. 'What did you do to break yours?'

'I think you're scaring him, Lindy,' said Eric.

Darkness filled the air as Lindy's face loomed over Nick; her open pores were filled in with make-up that was too dark for her complexion, defining an imaginary jawline. For an anxious moment he thought their eyes would lock, but she was quick and slid over his gaze as if it wasn't quite solid. She pulled the strand of hair from his mouth before proceeding towards Al, who'd curled into the shape of a question mark under his sheet.

'Where's my whip!' she shrieked. 'Where's my planet!' She pulled the curtain round Al's bed, and his bedside chair groaned when she sat in it. She kicked off her grubby pink stilettos and they were the only evidence of her, poking out from beneath the curtain.

Nick's head sank back into the pillow, his cheeks inflated with relief. Then the old man in the next bed coughed the kind of cough Nick associated with lonely park benches.

'Eric's the name, Nick.' Nick turned his head towards him. He was just a bunch of bones, held together by skin as thin as a condom and as blue as his bloodshot eyes. Eric was so old he had a gold tooth. Nick didn't want to talk; his body hurt every time he breathed and he had nothing to say. But he felt obliged; they were neighbours, and might be for some time.

'Where am I?'

It wasn't the question he'd meant to ask. He'd meant to ask what planet Lindy had lost, but had decided at the last moment that it could be one of those stupid, risky paths he was prone to take. Eric cackled with laughter. Across the divide, in the bed next to Al, another man gurgled.

'You're in the orthopaedic ward,' said Eric. 'We've all got something broken, except Al. He doesn't have anything broken this time, just a kidney problem, among other things.' He nodded at the man who'd gurgled, and around whose head was a steel halo, attached to his cheekbones. 'Bert fell off a roof and fractured his jaw and pelvis, and I fell off my chair and got a cracked neck-of-femur, among other things.' Eric surveyed the room. 'When you add it up, what with Bert's jaw wired shut and Al's natural reticence, you and I are the only ones capable of a conversation. But that's the nature of an orthopaedic ward.'

'Yeah, but what town am I in?'

'Marston.' Eric eyed him as if he were worse than a drifter; as if he were somebody cast adrift. 'They brought you in from Crundle, don't you remember?' Baring his flash gold tooth, he added, 'It's a tiny place, don't suppose there's much there to remember, these days.'

There was plenty to remember, but just then a trolley rattled in, pushed by a wiry wardsmaid in a pink uniform. The wardsmaid plonked a breakfast, hidden under a metal lid, on each man's steel bed trolley. Al's was whisked inside the curtain by Lindy. Her voice could be heard softly waffling to him, then suddenly a clang of the lid and she cried out. 'This egg's fried!'

The wardsmaid sighed, but stopped and waited as Lindy emerged from the curtain and stomped barefooted towards her with the offending plate.

'A boiled egg, please, Pat.'

Without a word, Pat lifted the lids of the rest of the trays until she found a boiled egg and exchanged it with Al's fried one. 'Anybody could poison an open egg like that,' Lindy said, bearing the egg back to Al. 'It's okay, Al,' she said, disappearing behind the curtain. 'We'll take the yolk out, and then it'll be all white and pure.'

Nick waited, but nobody came to feed him, so he stared out the window at a cow-shaped cloud that was floating belly-up. Yeah, he remembered Crundle. That was where he'd left Jude and the rest of his life, when all he'd meant to do was have a working holiday with his mate.

Someone was noisily scuffing down the corridor. A woman, skinny as a thread, stopped at the door to catch her breath. The antennae on her furry bumblebee slippers quivered as she shifted from foot to foot, gathering herself and darting curious glances at Nick from under a stringy fringe of hair.

'Lindy!' she called at last, darting towards Al's curtain. 'Mark's back.'

A burble came from behind the curtain.

The woman poked her head inside. 'Hi Al,' she said. 'You eating all right, hon?' The chair squeaked as Lindy rose. Her feet slid onto the stilettos; they were at least two sizes too small, overhung with great slabs of cracked heels.

The thin woman pulled back Al's curtain with a spindly hand, then tottered after Lindy sweeping towards the door. 'You'll never guess where he's been,' she said breathlessly, oblivious of Lindy's darkening face ahead of her. 'Or who he went with.' Her voice trailed down the hallway until it was cut short by Lindy's shriek for her whip.

'That was Trace,' said Eric, pulling the crusts off his toast. 'She and Lindy are thick as thieves – they'll have the whole bloody ward down here soon, visiting that poor bugger.'

Nick took stock of his situation. He was in a hospital in the wilds of Marston with a bunch of fruit loops. Staring at Al's shape under the sheet, he wondered how a guy with a kidney problem ended up in a broken bone ward, but decided the story would take longer than he wanted to listen.

'Who's Mark?' Nick asked.

'How would I know?' Eric snapped. 'I don't live here.'

The corridor came alive with footsteps, clacking with purpose and an impatient echo. Nick turned his head towards the door.

'Ah, lucky lad,' Eric muttered through his eggs. 'Here's our Nurse Sunni come to feed you.'

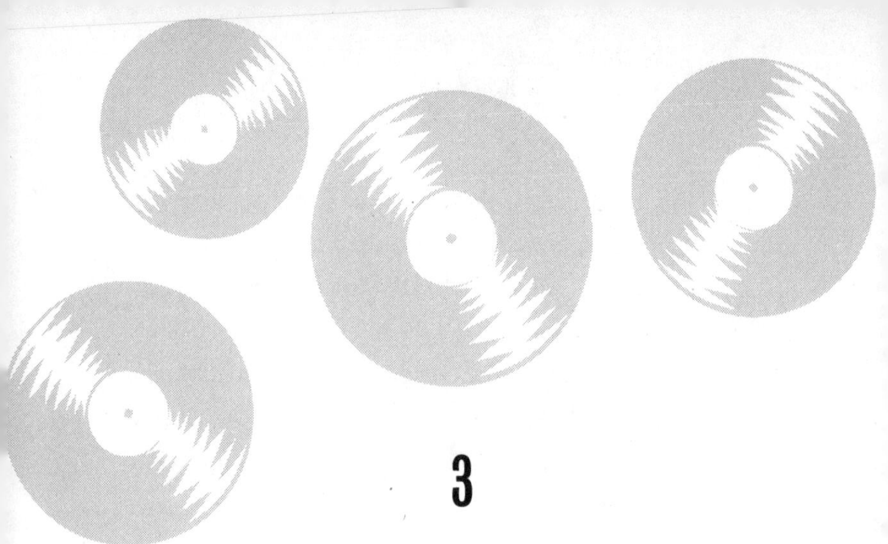

3

ONCE THERE WAS A LITTLE BROTHER AND A BEST MATE – AND then along came a girl.

𝄞

Nick tried to wake up, but the microphone kept falling from his hand. Caught in the dream, he was a singer on a stage. His joints had seized up and he'd forgotten the words to a song he'd never known anyway. His tongue thickened into cotton wool, his feet went numb. Watching the audience was like watching the enemy, and their sharp hisses soon pricked his feet back to life.

Bowie was at the end of the bed, plucking at his big toe.

'Wake up, wake up! You said you'd come to Time Warp with me.'

'I never said that. When did I say that?'

'You said it! You're leaving tomorrow. It's your last chance to kill Lola Starke.' The panic that had suffused Bowie's face was untainted by any trace of reason – it was so pure that Nick gave in without his usual resistance.

'Yeah, okay.' The singing dream retreated to the pit of his stomach, back where it belonged, until he figured out one day what to do with it. He rolled out of bed and lazily dressed, calling for Bowie to fish his new boots out from under the bed.

Sunday morning, and they stepped into the street, jammed with houses as cramped as theirs and with the same stunted palms and fishbone ferns gasping out front. Bowie waved cheerily to old Doris Hopper next door, on her knees in her patch of yard, butchering snails with a spade. He clomped beside Nick in outsized runners that made his legs look spindly. Cartoon legs, Nick teased. He liked Bowie, especially now, with his hot cheeks bright as a stop-button because it was Nick taking him out. Down the road they traipsed, Nick in his heavy new boots that would only get him as far as the bus stop, cursing Robbie for talking him into buying them. They were overtaken by muscular women running with dogs and prams, until they rounded the bay with its dogshit-studded embankment and its water smeary with boat drippings.

'They've got a new Lola game,' Bowie said, running up ahead and back and leaping around him. 'You'll really like it.'

'Yeah, yeah,' said Nick, keeping an eye on the kerb, keeping Bowie this side of it. At the bus stop Nick sat down and admired his new black boots while his toes curled with pain inside them. There'd be blisters, for sure; that's what you got for listening to Robbie's fashion sense.

Bowie gave up trying to make sense of the timetable, and used the pole as a pivot for his version of a pole-dance. 'Where will you sleep tomorrow?' he asked, swinging round to face Nick.

'I dunno. Maybe in a tree.' Nick feinted a lunge at him. 'Full of bloodthirsty yellow-bellied black snakes.'

'That's stupid. Snakes don't live in trees.' Bowie swung round the pole again. 'Maybe they live in ditches,' he said on his second turn. 'Or maybe they live at holiday camps.'

Nick looked away. 'Holiday camps are safe. No snakes, just tons of junk food and junky games. You'll have a great time.'

Bowie stopped spinning and came to stand in front of him. 'Nick? Why are you going away?'

'I'm not going away. I'm just taking a holiday.' *Not from you.* 'Everybody does it. You will too when you finish school.'

'When are you coming back?'

'Pretty soon.' *Head him off at the pass, don't meet his eyes.*

The bus approached. Bowie dug into his satchel and pulled out a container of one dollar coins.

'I brought my money and forgot my phone.'

'Well it's too late now and you won't need it. You're with me.'

On the bus Nick left Bowie to sit at the front while he sat down the back with Jonesy. Across the aisle two kids huddled over their knives. Nick could tell they were only jerk-off knives, so heavy their single use was to drop them on somebody's foot. He'd had one too, at their age. He'd loved the look of it and the promise of the weight in his hand – he'd imagined it would protect him from being a wimp. It didn't.

As the boys stood to get off the bus Nick leaned towards them. 'We know your names and we're gonna set the cops onto you.'

'Up yours,' the smaller one drawled as he meandered down the aisle.

'That's what my little brother could turn into,' Nick said to Jonesy. 'A cock-up with a blade.'

'So what? He's probably already got one – we did at ten.' Jonesy looked hard at Nick. 'Well, I did.'

'He's seven.'

Jonesy rolled his eyes. 'Maybe he's bright.'

Nick glanced down the aisle where Bowie sat dreamily in his cloudy little head. He was bright, but not in the way Jonesy meant.

'I saw your mate Robbie the other day,' Jonesy said. 'Says you're heading off to the bush.'

'Yeah, tomorrow. He's got an uncle with a farm and we'll pick peas or whatever it is he grows.'

'You call that a holiday?'

'A few months, get away from the folks, the kid-brother, and come back flush.'

'Yeah, the money,' Jonesy said. 'Bet you'd make more at a McCraps joint.'

'The idea is to get away, Jonesy, come back ready for uni, get a job . . .'

'Doing what?'

'Don't know.' That was the other reason he was heading off – he might find out what he could do, maybe even find out what he wanted.

Their stop came at Central Station and Jonesy gave him a farewell shove. Nick lurched down the aisle and cuffed Bowie on the shoulder.

'Get off, you berk.'

Time Warp was one of those downtown places good for killing a few hours if you liked that kind of thing. Nick used to, and now he didn't, but it had been his big-brother chore since Bowie had discovered his talent as a crack-shot a few months ago. He slouched in behind Bowie. Aside from the rising decibel level, nothing ever changed here; no girls, only a bunch of boys of all ages being heroes, aces and assassins.

Bowie's popularity was one of life's unsolved mysteries. He gladhanded a group of hoons gathered round a war game, and gave a friendly shriek over the gunfire and zaps to a beefy sharp-suited guy shooting at an animated version of himself.

'Bowie, mate.' The guy smiled with a sweetness that would have been frightening, Nick thought, if he were anywhere else but here. The guy was red-eyed, but his suit was too shiny, a dead giveaway. What was he doing, letting his little brother associate with these gun-slash-drug-runner types?

'This Lola's the best,' Bowie said, leading him to the machine. He fed her the money that would let him kill her if he was fast enough. 'I like her – she's really tricky.'

'Why do you want to kill her if you like her?' Nick asked. It was an unfair question, the same one that their father Cliff had asked him once, and which Nick had been unable to answer. He'd just sulked and moved on to another, deadlier game.

'That's what she's meant for.'

Why hadn't he thought of that?

Bowie went on, 'Only sometimes she's too smart.'

'You mean sometimes you're not quick enough.'

'No.' Bowie kept his eyes on the game. 'I'm the same. She figures out what she did wrong last time, and then she's ready for me.' He handed the game over to Nick, who played badly and half-heartedly, but it still rankled when Bowie wandered over to watch a kid play another game. The kid nodded without a pause, and Bowie stood behind encouraging him with 'yays' and shadow punches. Nick turned back to his game; Lola tossed him an eyeful of scorn and his hackles rose. *Get her.*

By the time he threw in the game she'd done him in eight times. He glanced around for Bowie, who'd moved on from the other kid. It wasn't such a big place that he couldn't scan it from where he stood, but there was no sight of Bowie. He checked his watch; he'd only played ten minutes so the kid couldn't be far. He went into the toilets and called Bowie's name, but nobody called back. There was no other room to check, and for a moment he simply stood, pushing down the panic butterflies and staring at the automatic entrance doors, the road, and all the other busy streets that ran off it in too many directions.

Bowie was a boy with a fast draw and a deadly aim, who'd get lost between the toilet and the bathtub. He was a dreamer, and he wandered while he dreamed. *Forward*, *up* and *down* were the directions he understood. If he couldn't toggle he was lost. He knew where he lived and he always had money to get there. That wasn't the point, it was never the point. The point was that Nick hadn't looked out for him, not now, and not earlier when they should've gone back for the phone. Here he was, on the eve of his great adventure, and he'd gone and lost his little brother.

The butterflies would not be stilled as Nick imagined Bowie crossing roads, entering buildings with rear exits into lanes that descended into alleys and ended up as drains. He checked his watch again. Two minutes had elapsed. At most, Bowie had been gone twelve minutes. *Find him – but which way*?

Nick worked the room, asking the kid, the hoons, the guy at the next machine and the next.

'Bowie?' The gun-runner bared his smiley teeth. 'How ya doin', Bowie?' he yelled, turning away.

'No, I'm his brother!' Nick shouted back. 'I'm looking for him.'

'Mate, I'm *talking* to him. He's behind the machine.'

'What the . . .' Nick gawked at the guy with disbelief before peering into the recess between the machine and the wall.

'Dropped his coins and they rolled under the machines along this wall,' the guy said. 'He'll have picked up most of them by now.'

Only a runt like Bowie would fit in that space – and there he was, head down, bum up, one arm probing under the machine. Nick would have lunged at him, but all he could do was bellow into Bowie's startled face.

'Get out of there!'

'Just two more and I've got them all.'

Nick waited, relieved and pissed off, but more relieved. 'I'm late for a date,' he explained to the bemused gun-runner. When Bowie emerged with his rescued coins, Nick grunted at him and steered him towards the door.

'Nick?'

'What now?'

'If you knew someone was going to die and they were never coming back, would you love them?' It was a reasonable, seven-year-old question, and Nick refrained from scoffing.

'Lola dies,' he said, 'and you like her.'

'But she keeps coming back – that's why I love her.'

'I dunno,' Nick said. 'You'd still love Mum if she died.'

'But we already love her. I mean would you *start* to love them?'

'Why are you asking?'

'Well, I really want that spotty puppy, the one Dad said was worse than a runt. He said he would die so I shouldn't set my heart on him.'

'If that's the one you want . . .'

'I do!' Bowie cried as the doors opened. 'But what if he dies?'

'I don't know . . . you might have to take the risk.' They stepped into the street and Bowie turned left. Just as Nick went to whistle him back, Bowie turned around and threw up his hands in mock horror.

'Yeah,' said Nick. 'This way, you dork.'

𝄞

Fingers of early morning light slid across the road to where Robbie's car idled, a white Toyota, sturdy, battered and old enough to be easily and cheaply fixed. Robbie sat at the wheel with his head cocked, listening for ticks in the engine. They were ready to go, with only the formalities to get through. Nick grinned up at his mother, Maree, who was hunched over the passenger window. Her face was yellowish and haggard, still recovering from last night's shift at the restaurant. Her fingers, one of which was bandaged, drummed the sill while she delivered her instructions.

'I know you're no longer a schoolboy. I know you've got a place to go to. And if you don't call tonight I'll set the police onto you.' She poked her head inside the car. 'You hear me, Robbie?'

'Mum, you said all this last night . . .' Nick hissed.

'You're the senior one here, Robbie,' Maree went on. Nick turned to inspect Robbie's sudden maturity. Only a year between them, but Robbie always got older faster than he did.

'You call your mother tonight, and make sure Nick calls me. Then you can email, I can't read that SMS.'

'We'll call.' Robbie gave her his reassuring smile, so practiced it was oily and she surely wouldn't fall for it. But he immediately followed it up with his lopsided grin, and Maree went around to his window. She reached in and patted his hand, which was clutching the wheel, twitching to go. The bulges in her forearms, from lifting half a cow, or a dozen chickens from the oven, reminded Nick of how strong she was, and the permanent burn across her wrist reminded him how hazardous it was being a chef.

Cliff, mild-eyed and leafy-browed, emerged from the front door in his pyjamas. He stepped over old Lois's balding tail and managed a wave that was both vigorous and vague. 'Dad looks like he's calling the rains down,' Nick murmured. Robbie gunned the engine while he contemplated Nick's father.

'My guess is he thinks he's waving to you. You're both the same, blokes with bad aims.'

Bowie was the one with the deadly aim, Nick thought, watching him leap past Cliff and run down the path. He grabbed hold of the belt of Maree's gown, jumping like a jackhammer. Maree caught him and held him close. They both gave Nick smiles with no trace of reproach. Nick grinned inanely into the middle distance and waited for her to stand aside and give them passage to the world. At last she did.

'Your mum's not real happy about you going,' Robbie said when they turned the corner.

'She worries about Bowie, that's all.'

'She worries about you,' Robbie said. 'Bowie will survive the holiday camp, same as we did.'

'We knew where we were.'

'Spare me the clucking hen bit,' Robbie said as he pulled up at a red light. 'He's getting a new puppy to play with, and you'll be chucked on the scrap heap with poor old Lois.'

The girl in the Astra beside them was using her rear-vision mirror to drowsily apply mascara. The light turned green and nobody moved. 'Here we are,' Robbie said, 'heading into the wilds and the first thing we hit is a bottleneck on Broadway.' They settled down to watch the girl in the Astra set up her make-up bag on the dash and pull out a tube of lipstick.

'Beats camp,' Nick said, his mouth opening slightly as she slicked a crimson stick over her already glossy lips. She was sleek and smooth and showed no interest in Nick when she glanced over, but lingered a moment on Robbie. Robbie, cool as always, didn't gaze back, though Nick knew he'd have taken in every visible detail of her. Robbie wore his lust like a velvet coat. Most of the time Nick thought he bore his own like a toothache.

4

NURSE SUNNI ENTERED THE WARD ON HER DAILY CHECK FOR signs of life.

Dr Hilton, who'd been assigned to Nick, was still on his afternoon rounds. He tapped the concrete around Nick's leg before delivering his verdict. 'The metal rod is screwed into the bone to secure and stabilise it.'

'How long am I going to be part of this contraption?' Nick asked him.

'About five weeks.'

Nick blanched with shock. The doctor turned to address Nurse Sunni's bowed head. 'These are the injuries most likely to occur in a minor accident. The victim extends his hands to protect the face.'

Apparently resigned to being a substitute medical student, Nurse Sunni looked up from her chart with a vacant clinical stare. Dr Hilton nodded approvingly, swung round to take

Nick by the jaw, and continued his lecture. 'Concussion and lacerations to the face and head demonstrate the complete ineffectiveness of such action.' He tapped Nick on the forehead. 'The patient wasn't wearing a helmet. He's lucky he hit a signpost and not another vehicle. Lucky to be alive. He's a big strong boy. It's a pity his sense didn't match. Right, next patient.'

Nick knew humiliation when it was handed to him, and it did not abate when Nurse Sunni's cool fingers put the thermometer into his ear. She took his pulse, smiling to herself, keeping count of the throbs that must have told her how fat his dick was getting. Nothing he could do about it.

'It's only hormones,' Nurse Sunni said, writing on his chart. 'Nothing to do with your mind.' Spic and span in her crisp white shirt, there was no shadow of a crease in its glare. It was a uniform – reassuring in this place of weird get-ups – and he longed for her to be kind to him, to treat him like a person. Her eyes were lowered, but he could still read the acid in them: *all this pain, it's nobody's fault but yours.*

'Put that leg down,' she ordered, picking the sheet off the floor where he'd kicked it. 'Or you'll break it too.' Nurse Sunni's voice was sharp at the edge, reaching into tight corners, flicking out insubordination. He plonked his left leg down. Maybe his balls were dangling, but only Nurse Sunni would tell him to do something about it. 'No need to be sulky,' she said. Maybe that passed for kindness.

Bert emitted one of his gurgles. Nick ignored it. There was etiquette here: he wasn't obliged to talk to the patients on the other side of the room. He'd been here four days now, and Eric sounded like he'd never been any place else. Even Al seemed to bear the stupefying desolation simply by staring at the ceiling. So far, Al hadn't spoken, but he was from Lindy's ward, and Nick soon learnt that his feeble wave the other day was just his way of clearing the air of contaminants.

Nick watched Nurse Sunni's retreating legs. They were made for fishnet stockings, like the ones Jude once wore for a gig. Trashy, Jude had called them, and when she'd let him roll them down he could only agree. *Can't go there, the road's closed.* He sighed heavily.

'She's pretty, that Sunni,' Eric said. 'You might think she's nice, but don't go mooning after her just because she treats you like you're still alive. She's doing her job, that's all. We're her job, shaving us, wiping our arses, and she doesn't get paid enough for it so don't expect any favours.'

'I'm not mooning over her – she's mean. But at least she's not part of the freak show.'

'Her loss.' Eric folded his arms and checked the clock over the door.

It was four o'clock. Eric had a wife, Iris, and she was dead on time, padding through the door in her soft jiffy slippers and tan cardigan. Iris murmured her complaints about the weather, the traffic and how long it took to get here, and Eric grunted into the woolly spaces between her words.

Order came to the world when Iris pulled out a rolled-up *Daily Courier* and *Women's Weekly* from her navy blue plastic handbag, and shook the creases out of the paper before giving it to Eric. She dragged the chair round to Nick's side of the bed, to be closer to the window and the sky. With a kind of dazed enthralment she watched a pearly ball of light break a hole in the clouds. 'Lovely,' she said when the show was over. She put on her reading glasses and picked up the magazine, her lower lip quivering as she turned the pages from the back cover to the front. Finally she settled down to read the lot from the beginning, while Eric looked the other way and slipped his hand into her bag, the way he did every day. Nick watched him pull out the small brown folder, the kind you put cards or pictures in. Opening it, Eric pored over whatever was there for a long time before sliding it back into the bag. Iris never gave him a second glance.

At five o'clock on the dot, Iris silently mouthed the words in the ad on the back cover. She put the magazine on Eric's bed, pecked him on the ridge of his cheekbone and patted the ghost of his hair. 'Tooroo, love,' she said to Nick on her way out. In a rage Eric flapped the magazine at the empty doorway.

'Don't leave me with this bloody rubbish!' He flopped back into the pillows, coughing from the exertion of yelling. 'Nurse! I need a sputum mug!'

Five o'clock and the night was already coming on. Nick

dreaded it. The night brought the hum of machinery. Machines were everywhere, some keeping bodies alive, who didn't want to be; others not doing enough for bodies clinging to every throb. At night Nick could hear them all, and those he couldn't, he imagined. The nurses wandered around like zombies at four in the morning, the hour they sterilised the instruments and the bedpans, and the hour Nick screamed for his pain-killer; the death hour, they liked to tell him, when the body was at its lowest ebb, so don't push it. Then came the dawn-whine of polishers, the hollow ring of emptied buckets, and at last the soft swish of mops that sent him back to sleep.

The others arrived, as Eric had said they would. Shepherded by Lindy, who'd brought Eric a bowl to spit in, the patients from Al's ward filed in, doing their daily visit. Nick had waited, but no bad-boy called Mark had shown up and nobody mentioned his name. Maybe Mark was Lindy and Trace's delusion. Nick watched everyone flit around Al. They complained to each other about their medications, their doctors, their therapy. If they didn't complain they compared, as if doctors and medication was stuff they could get on mail order and return within ten days.

A man was telling Trace, 'I called my doctor and . . . he said he wouldn't come.'

'It was four in the morning, Victor. You called yourself Elvis.'

'Then . . . he knew it was me.'

Trace patted Victor's hand. 'Hon, we're the chronics. Nobody's going to come at four in the morning for us.' She turned to Nick and whispered loudly, 'We don't get treated anymore, we get maintained.'

Victor sloped over to stand by Nick's bed, where he carefully combed his ducktail in the reflection of the window. He put the comb into the pocket of his narrow silver pants and stepped back, admiring his hair. He swivelled his hips awkwardly and pushed them towards Nick. 'Do I look like . . . Elvis?' he asked.

'Sure, mate – the thin version.'

Victor's nearly toothless smile was angelic, but four days was enough time for the glamour of craziness to wear off. It turned out they were just people – people he had to interact with. He'd tried to resist, but couldn't help hearing as they filled Al in on the dramas of their ward; who was fighting, who was reconciled, and who the aligned were – which Nick figured was wardspeak for who was sharing their bed between ward rounds. Al never responded, but Lindy could read the angles of his legs, glean nuance from his blank eyes. His knees were always up, and he appeared to be in a permanent state of recoil from some horror. All his visitors, though, knew when to ignore him, when to pat his hand and when to pull the sheet over and leave him curled up alone.

When Victor pulled out a cigarette, Nurse Sunni magically appeared. 'Don't you dare.' Victor kept the cigarette in his mouth, but put the lighter back in his pocket. 'You'll kill yourself with those things,' she told him. Victor removed the cigarette and spoke through gritted teeth.

'I'll think about that when I . . . get well.'

'You won't get well here. Back to your own room! Go on, all of you.'

'We're visitors, we've got a right to be here,' Lindy said. 'And Al's got a right to see us.'

'Al's not seeing very much at all,' said Nurse Sunni.

'No, not even his doctor,' Lindy complained. 'He just up and went on holiday to Surfers.'

'Dr Buckle is covering,' Nurse Sunni said briskly. 'Now shoo!'

Lindy rolled her eyes. The others trooped out for their smoko, waved off by Eric. Only Lindy was the stayer. When they'd gone, she opened the drawer in Al's locker, pulled out a chocolate bar and ate it thoughtfully. Their ward was a kind of club. None of them, though, appeared to know about Lindy's stash of chocolates. Everybody has secrets, even club members, Nick thought, blinking in the sudden silence.

Nurse Sunni brought him a message slip. 'Your friend Robbie called. He'll be over to see you in a couple of days.'

'About time,' Nick muttered.

'He's been before, when you were admitted. You were

unconscious.' She cranked his bed up to the eating position, then trotted out when a bell rang in the corridor.

Dinner came, delivered by the wiry Pat. Eric lifted the lid hopefully, but drew back. 'Pap,' he said, dropping the lid onto the plate.

'Maybe it's Al's.'

'Not his, this is brown.' He lifted a spoonful and let it dribble back onto the plate. 'Oh, wait a minute – there's a sausage here.' He speared it and waved it consolingly at Nick. 'Chin up, she'll be back to feed you.'

'Oh! God!'

It was Lindy. Everyone held their breath as she grabbed Al's plate and charged to the doorway, blocking it before Pat could make an exit. Lindy presented the plate of white fish in white sauce to Pat and addressed the top of her puffy disposable hat.

'There's a speck.'

Pat inspected the plate. 'It's a pea.'

Lindy drew herself to her full height to make her pronouncement. 'Exactly. Al's food has to be *pure* white so he can find the contaminations. You know they're trying to poison him.'

Pat took a clean knife from her trolley and flicked out the pea. Lindy ground it into the lino with her stiletto. She was fast, she was heavy, and she didn't need a whip.

'You're so right, babe,' she said, bearing the plate back to Al. 'It's the only way to catch them at it.' She sat without drawing the curtain, took a mouthful and joined his gaze on the ceiling. 'You don't eat it anyway, babe. You'll always be safe.'

Al quietly starved, Bert Jawframe sucked on his eggflip, and Eric, who'd bolted his down to avoid too much flavour, flipped through the *Women's Weekly* Iris had left him. Nick could see the luscious scarlet lips on the front cover and he silently mouthed, the way Iris did, the slogan: *put your money where your mouth is.* At the top of the magazine was a blue ink stamp that said 'Shelley's Pathology Do Not Remove'. Iris got the magazines from all over town, but the best ones, the ones with the extra-thick, stiff, glossy covers, came from Noreen's Beauty Salon. Nick was up on his magazine covers, seeing as he couldn't turn the pages.

'Dinner's on,' Trace called to Lindy from the doorway.

'I'll be a minute.' While Lindy finished Al's dinner and filled him in on the latest developments between two addicts named Doug and Michelle, Trace flitted over to Nick.

'They've forgotten you, hon?' She lifted the lid on his dinner. 'May as well earn me keep. Yum! Open up, it's bangers and mash.' She cut up the entire sausage, as if for a child, then speared a piece and held it up. The fork and sausage segment quivered in her shaky hand as she brought them to his mouth. Then he copped a whiff of the nicotine on her fingers, and his lips clamped shut.

For four days he'd been festering, had hardly said a word

and nobody had noticed. All these visitors, none of them were his, and it was all his own fault. He slept and woke with remorse; he had more remorse than he'd ever need. Sooner or later he was going to pay for what he'd done, but not by having a frantically cheery, chain-smoking loony tune try to feed him.

'Piss off.'

Hurt collapsed Trace's placid face. She dropped the fork onto the plate and shuffled in her bumblebee slippers to stand by Lindy. Lindy wiped her lips with a tissue and put Al's plate back on the tray. She stood up, brushing aside Trace on her way to Nick's bed. He watched her approach, his rising resentment tasting like impotence. He wasn't puny, but he would have drawn back from her if he could. Captive in his plaster, he thought he could withstand her verbal abuse, but if she hit him he was a goner.

'Who loves you, Nick?' she breathed gently.

Her question was cruel, and his mind went blank as he stared at her long black eyes. He looked around the room. Bert and Eric had their ears cocked, waiting, he knew, to hear what 'the little shit' could come up with. Who loved him? He didn't have to answer – this was crazy. His gaze turned back to Lindy. He did have to answer it. He'd had a person who put her trust in him; she would have loved him, all he had to do was be true. If he hadn't given her a reason to run, they'd have come through it together. 'Not Jude,' he said to himself.

'That's who doesn't love you,' Lindy said, startling him.

Nick appealed to Trace. 'Did I speak?' Trace nodded. He went back to thinking. Her dogs didn't love him either. Aside from the folks, who didn't have much choice, the only sure thing was Bowie. But he wasn't going to tell that to the giant troll leering over him, or her lackey hiding behind her skirt.

'My little brother loves me.'

'You've got a little brother?' Trace squeaked. 'You are *so* lucky.'

Though he hadn't asked for it, her smile was one of utter forgiveness. Nothing lasted long here, not even rancour. Lindy lobbed her a look of disapproval.

'You're too easy, Trace.'

With Trace in her wake Lindy accepted the *Women's Weekly* Eric handed to her on her way out, leaving Nick with his mouth clamped again.

When their footsteps had receded down the hallway, Eric listed towards him. 'You're young and obviously stupid, given the nature of your injuries, but you can't treat people like that when they're only being kind.'

'It just came out, I didn't mean it – and she got over it.'

'Listen to yourself. You act badly and think you can explain it away as if it never happened, cocky as a blue-eyed bat.' Eric slumped into the pillows. 'Then you think you're free to do it again.'

'I just wanted some privacy,' he said, wincing at the sulkiness in his voice. It wasn't true; he didn't know what he wanted. But now he'd gone and set Eric off. The old man was pulling his bones up in the bed, trying to sit higher, and alarming Nick with the profusion of spittle gathering around his mouth. Enough to reach him if he decided to spit it out.

'You think privacy's a right? Who's been pulling the wool over your eyes? You and me, we've got no privacy – those nurses know our arseholes better than we'll ever know them.'

'There are other kinds of privacy . . .'

'What kind were you after? Privacy's the privilege of the privileged. You and me, we don't get privileges. Look at this place. Al over there's a renal case with a head problem and I'm a respiratory case, both of us in an orthopaedic ward.'

'You've got a broken hip.'

'Minor detail,' he spluttered. 'Nowadays you get put where there's a bed. If you die because they haven't got the right equipment in the ward, too bad. At least you get to die in a bed, what more do you want?' He spat into his bowl.

Nick stared at his wild old eyes.

'Bit of a radical, were you?'

Eric threw him a look of disgust. 'Are, not were,' he said, sinking so far back into the pillows that he looked in danger of suffocating. 'I'm a realist.' Then his head flew up again and Nick, even from his distance, got a whiff of his volcanic breath. 'What have you ever done for society?'

Nick pondered. 'I went to an anti-gun rally once,' he said at last. It was a long time ago and Maree had dragged him along, kicking and screaming. That was about the time she'd found his jerk-off knife.

'Fighting for peace, rooting for virginity.' When Eric spat into his bowl, Nick took it as hostile action.

'So, Eric,' he drawled. 'What did you find to do for society?'

'I've done without.' He turned to face the door, finished with Nick.

Eric was being cryptic, fishing, not for an audience – he already had a captive one – but for a spark of interest. Nick could've asked what he was talking about. Instead, he used his chin to press the lever for the nurses' call button. There was a little pellet of contrition in his craw, but while he'd take back what he'd said to Trace if he could, what he needed now was a shit, not a lecture from a cranky old radical.

As if he'd heard Nick's thought, Eric said, 'Have you got any idea what an ignorant waster you are?'

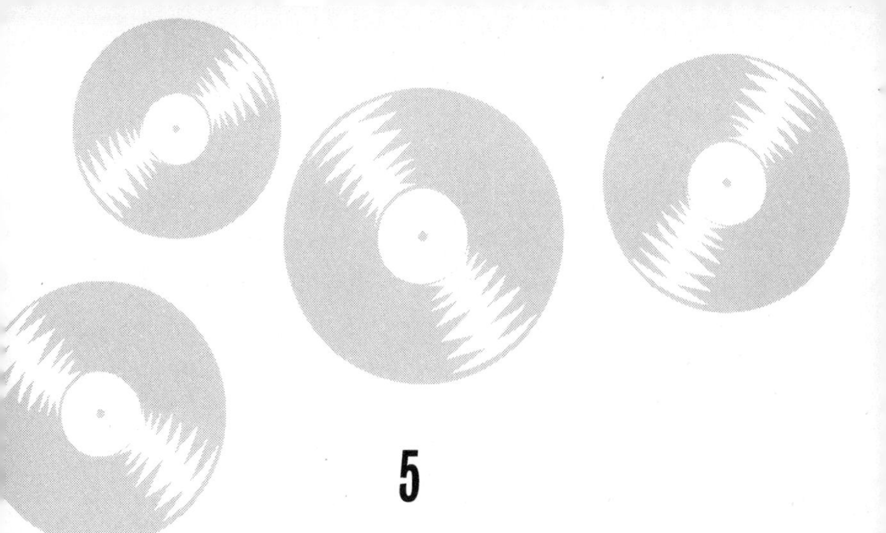

5

NICK AND ROBBIE WERE ON THE ROAD. NICK TRIED TO BE blasé about it, but the anticipation of setting out, the hopes for what might lie on the way, kept surfacing as half-baked laughs, punctuated by the acidic jazz that Robbie had playing on the tape. He'd never been so far from the city, had never been further than commuting distance to the sea. When they were kids, Robbie used to disappear to Crundle during school holidays. But for Nick, drives out of the city with Cliff and Maree had meant three hours up the coast, or the short trip up the mountains, but never over the other side. Even that distance was too far from Cliff's comfort zone. There were plenty of city parks to lark around in, he'd say, if you want your fill of green. And if it was space you wanted, you only had to go to Bondi and look east.

The sun was breaking through the silvery mist when they crossed the mountains. Nick and Robbie were leaving the past with the eastern seaboard, and steadily heading west. For a time there had been trees – wattles, gums, and others whose botanical names Robbie had rattled off and Nick had promptly forgotten. When the trees gave out Robbie identified the mondo grasses, button and kerosene grasses, none of which Nick could distinguish, though he liked the names. By the time they stopped to piss he was overloaded with names, and the grass they stood in was anonymous, knee high, ticking with grasshoppers and cloudy with gnats. Nick took aim at the lowest twigs on a straggly roadside shrub, washing off the dust to give the tiny furred leaves a little breathing space.

Back in the car Nick took the wheel while Robbie climbed over the back to sleep off last night's farewell. He changed the music to hip-hop and finished the sandwiches they'd bought at the last petrol station, an outpost with a bowser so decrepit they'd been able to take a breath between each click of the gauge. Nick's sandwich had tasted just as old, but that could have been the heat, and each hour was getting steadily hotter.

Wind, heat and dust. Somebody must have written a song about it, and it was a small price for driving on an open road, alone, but for Robbie snoozing in the corner and a passing car every fifty klicks. The road felt like a threshold, stretching all the way to the horizon where his future tapped its toes, waiting for him to catch up. He couldn't decide whether jangling bebop or racy hip-hop would suit his raging melancholy, so he settled on Roy Orbison, his eternal favourite. Roy could make his voice do anything – turn the air misty with laments, cut paper, release adrenaline or out-twinkle a starry night in the desert.

Nick listened and sang and dreamed of being a heart-breaking singer.

By late afternoon Robbie was back at the wheel. Nick had his bare feet bolstering the windscreen and was staring between them at the bald grey hills looming on the horizon. The land was relentlessly grim, with a chorus line of bill-boards for the last few kilometres of the approach to Marston. Lined up in parched, stubbled paddocks, they advertised tractors, pesticides, Cow Radio, sheep dip and a list of the services in Marston, the town that crouched behind the shadowy hills.

'It's only an hour to Crundle,' Robbie told him as they drove through Marston's sprawling main street. It was lined with stock agents, milk bars, butchers and pubs, newsagents and Wall's Emporium, interspersed with downmarket chain stores. They circled a roundabout from which a trophy palm tree sprouted, surrounded by a green wrought-iron fence.

'This is the big town – the one we hit Saturday nights,' Robbie said, stopping to let two girls cross the road. One of them languidly lifted her hand in thanks, glanced through the windscreen and copped the full whack of Robbie's easy smile.

She tittered the way Nick had seen countless girls do, and suddenly changed her casual walk into a self-conscious strut.

'How do you do it?' Nick murmured.

'You're asking me?' Robbie said it smugly, as if he hadn't made dozens of girls fall in love with him.

'Yeah, I am. What about Emma?' Robbie hadn't had to do a thing to make Emma switch her attentions from Nick to him except wear his smile and appear to be full of the secrets girls wanted whispered to them.

'I did you a favour there,' Robbie said. 'That girl's area manager of McCraps now – she's going places you'd fear to tread.'

'She always had ambition and common sense,' Nick agreed grudgingly. 'I kind of hoped she'd lose the common sense when she was with me – be a bit wild.'

'And I spared you the pain of finding out there was no hope at all,' Robbie said, stepping on the gas as they reached the end of town.

Not for the first time, Nick wondered whether he hung around Robbie just to pick up some of that whizzbang light of the blue-eyed boy, and whether Robbie just liked having someone to reflect it back onto him. As usual, the answer was a mental shrug followed by a maybe, yes, sometimes, but they'd been mates all their lives and though the Emma thing chafed at his pride there'd been other factors to brace the friendship.

'Did you bring enough books to get you through?' he asked.

Robbie's eyes rolled at Nick's question. 'Did you bring enough music?'

Nick grunted.

On the other side of the town the signs of progress began to peter out; the road got narrower, the trees sparser and the few billboards were all facing the other way. There was no evidence of a river, not even a trickle of a creek. They were surrounded by a horizon where a stampede of wild horses, spooked cattle or a posse of rampaging drovers could appear at any moment. Nick turned to look through the back window. So this was what happened when you left a country town – whichever way you turned it was all west. He could see no bounds to the plain, only the big sky rolling over at the end of a hard day, exposing its underbelly to the sinking sun.

'Do you get used to all this space?' he asked Robbie.

'I haven't been here since I was eleven – I loved it, but I never got used to it.' He glanced out his window. 'It's beautiful, and you know me – I'm addicted to beautiful.'

The air was turning cooler, seemed less dusty. They were approaching a river, heralded by a line of trees floating on the horizon, where the sun was getting ready to set; then came willows and glimpses of black still water.

The front tyre burst as they entered Crundle, just before the petrol station.

'Funny, that,' Robbie said, inspecting a shred of rubber. As they pushed the car to the workshop he said, 'You reckon they sprinkle tacks around?'

'Don't need them with these stones,' Nick muttered, regretting that he hadn't pulled his boots back on.

'I got another job to finish,' the mechanic told them. 'Then I'm closing up shop. Yours'll be ready tomorrow morning. The pub's up on Hill Street, if you want a room.'

Robbie turned to Nick. 'Might as well check out the pub. Tony can pick us up from there.'

The mechanic nodded at Nick's bare feet. 'I'd put some shoes on mate, a lot of tacks out there.'

After Nick pulled on his boots they stood on the verge of Crundle. 'It's just like I remember,' Robbie said as they trudged into a hamlet of two straggly intersecting streets. A few mulberry trees and worn-out wattles lined the one they were moseying down, past Harry's Feed Store, Sid's Café and Shirley's Hardware, all closed at seven o'clock. At irregular intervals side lanes veered off and dwindled away after a few metres when the houses, and any reason to continue, ceased.

When they reached the main intersection Nick contemplated the rise with dismay. Hill Street was long and ridiculously steep. His feet hurt already. 'Why would you plonk the pub up there?'

'Pubs weren't on my radar back then,' Robbie said. 'I only

remember cows, tractors, plants and bugs. And the pink milkshakes at Sid's.'

Nick took out his mobile, but it was dead.

'Another reason to head up the hill,' said Robbie. 'We'll get a signal up there. Let's go.' After sitting in a car all day, they both needed the stretch even if they didn't want it. They heaved their way past a scattering of shopfronts that were either boarded up or pasted with newspaper. When they passed a man sleeping on flattened cartons in the entrance of Beulah's Books, Nick said, 'You do all that reading, why don't you do an arts degree?'

'No money in it.' Robbie inspected the peeling sign and then the sleeping guy whose ginger beard was beginning to turn grey. 'He probably owns that shop.' Just the kind of answer Nick expected from a guy who'd forced Literature onto him from the age of ten, who'd used it as bait: *if you talk to me about* Lord of the Flies, *I'll listen to your whining Roy Orbison.* And then moves on to something completely unrelated.

'But why horticulture?' Nick said. 'All that gets you is a job weeding parks.'

'It's what I want.' Robbie pushed him ahead. 'Get a move on, I'm thirsty.'

They rose above the ghost end of the street to the hum of life and the lights at the top. Finally they scaled the summit and limped towards the pub, a low timber building squatting next to its crammed car park. The pub's verandah roof extended over the footpath, and a brightly painted tin sign hung from its eaves. *The Fat Stag*. Nick laughed at the name and the stout buck prancing above the words. He was still laughing when his gaze fell on a young woman with long dark hair tied back with a red bandanna. She was sitting on the kerb beneath the sign, and she was flanked by two grey dogs as thin as midday shadows. Her arm was around one dog's neck, and she talked to it while the other dog listened in. At the sound of Nick's laughter she looked up at him with a tender sleepy smile. Her heavy hair swung a little. Nick stared at her, the dogs glared at Nick, and Robbie emitted a whoop.

'Hey, Jude,' he said. 'They make you earn your beer round here.'

'It's the old church,' she said, gently probing the dog's neck. 'And we still do penance – only now it's before we sin.' Her voice slowed to a drawl. 'But that only counts for those who still have to walk up the hill. Strangers mostly, and a few unfortunates.' When Robbie chuckled at her mock Gothic tone she laughed with him, clear-eyed and sparkly, before continuing her inspection of the dog's neck.

Nick kept staring at her. The weakness in his legs was nothing, a physical reaction from tackling the hill, though the sudden ache in his chest unsettled him. Nothing he couldn't push down, he thought, watching her pull a creature from the dog's neck, hold it up and squash it between her fingers.

'Ticks,' she said, reaching for the other dog. 'You remember ticks, Robbie?'

'Like my own family.' He gestured at Nick. 'This is Nick, we'll be staying at Tony's, do some picking for him.'

'Hello, Nick,' she said.

'Jude.' He nodded.

Robbie shoved him and started for the bar door. 'See you inside, Jude.'

'I'm heading off,' she said. 'I just came to sort out a gig I'm doing here.'

Robbie turned, his face alight with surprised pleasure. 'You mean all those years of hitting me with Mongolian folk songs have paid off. When are you on?'

'Wednesday – rockabilly night. I'm on, along with the rest of the town. I've been doing it a while, and only at the Stag, so don't be too impressed.' She turned to Nick. 'Everybody gets to sing here – it's the local version of karaoke.'

'C'mon, Nick, we gotta call your mummy and my Uncle Tony.' Robbie nudged him and headed though the swinging saloon doors to the bar. Nick's weak laugh seemed to make Jude's smile widen a little.

'See you Wednesday, then,' he said to her, hoping he sounded cool. *When did a squeak ever sound cool?*

'Her father was a friend of Tony's,' Robbie said when they got their drinks. 'Had an olive farm out woop-woop and he'd bring her over to play with me sometimes. Haven't seen her since we were ten – I think her mother got sick. She's grown up all right, eh?' He downed his beer and looked at Nick's empty glass. 'You want another Coke?'

Nick shook his head. 'Let's wait for Tony outside.'

Outside night had fallen, and with it came great fat stars like he'd never seen before, millions of them flourishing in nothing more than thin air.

6

AT NIGHT NICK'S PAIN TOOK ON AN EXTRA DIMENSION. IT felt like someone in hobnailed boots was stomping around in the space between the plaster and his skin.

'What do you *want*?' The night nurse, exasperated, hovered at the door.

'I don't know! Some help, stronger painkillers, something . . .'

'Your medication isn't due for an hour.'

'It never works.'

'Then you'll just have to bear it.'

'I can't.'

'Mate . . .' Eric began, but the sympathy in his voice only made Nick more aware of his helplessness, and the tears of frustration draining into the corners of his mouth tasted like despair.

Most nights, though, Eric slept through it, and on these

nights Nick conducted one-sided conversations with Al. Bert didn't talk, but only because his jaw was wired. Al's silence was a mystery, an absence that Nick took refuge in when fragments of thoughts crashed about in his head like drunken bees. When Eric and Bert's snores muffled the mechanical noises and the sound of Nick's voice, he'd talk softly to Al. 'How's it going, Al?' Al never answered, and in the end Nick would give up. 'Not too good, mate.' He'd stare out the window, at the barely perceptible brightening of the moonlight as the long nights accumulated.

In the morning Phil hoisted Nick up into the eating position. Phil was small, pale and strong. He'd lifted Nick a number of times, and Nick felt that he was no more trouble to him than a leaf. Phil let out a bellow when he straightened up, and Nick figured that was where his strength lay.

It was a relief when Phil came back to feed him his lunch. Unlike Nurse Sunni, Phil's bedside manner didn't take a dive each time he inserted the spoon into Nick's mouth. There was enough time between Phil's spoonfuls to talk about football.

'How about that Wally!' Phil said.

'What?'

'Last night's game.' For a moment Phil was baffled, then his face cleared. 'You'll have to hire a TV.'

'I don't need a TV,' Nick told him. 'Not that I'm not a fan.' *I can't afford a TV.* 'But you could always re-enact the tries for me.'

Phil nodded doubtfully and fed him his painkillers. Nurse Sunni was strong and efficient, but Phil was strong and gentle. It was nothing to do with personality; it was in the hands, the touch – it was a lesson Nick was learning.

Phil ventured over to see how Al was doing, but Al shooed him away with his spoon, as he did with all the nurses.

'Where's Lindy?' Nick asked. 'She's never missed a meal before.'

'I don't know.' Bending over Nick, Phil whispered, 'Maybe she preferred another patient's lunch.' He straightened and made for the door.

'Phil?' Nick said. 'Where does it say on my chart that my parents are out of the country?'

'It doesn't,' he said. 'That kind of information isn't recorded here.'

That Lindy must have a spy ring going.

While he waited for the painkillers to work, Nick joined Eric in watching the clock. Three more hours before Iris arrived. As outside life retreated with the passing days, Nick looked forward to Iris's visits. She was one of those old women he would never have noticed unless they fell on him in the bus, but who was hard to ignore on her home turf. The way she sat in the plastic chair by Eric's bed, reading magazines as if she were passing time on her own front porch, the hospital was clearly home turf to Iris. The muffled sweep of newsprint and the flick of glossy pages were the only sounds she and Eric exchanged; the two of them together, in cahoots, was strangely reassuring; the way Eric's fingers went for her purse and sometimes missed, slipping into Iris's hand instead. When Iris was here, Eric was entirely bearable. With that last thought, Nick realised that the painkillers were kicking in.

Heels sparked down the corridor, accompanied by a peppery smell Nick recognised, but couldn't name. He knew there would be no visitors for him, but the familiar smell triggered anticipation and a little thrill of fear as the footsteps slowed at the ward door. Maybe Robbie had caved in and told Maree, and now she and her hysteria were stomping in to yell at him – she would attack on the grounds he was her eldest son and should know better than to get himself mixed up with a girl who had whips. *Whippets*, he'd tell her. *Dogs, Mum*. The steps passed, but Nick was already tangled up in the conversation with his mother: *You wouldn't have liked her*, he'd say, just so he wouldn't have to give away pieces of Jude. And Maree would say, *I might have*. Her voice would be thin with weariness, and he would be able to see her skin aching and her bones creaking as she limped to his bedside after a hard day's cooking at the restaurant. And now that he was a regular reader of *Woman's Day*, courtesy of Iris, he could have told her that it was probably only the wrong colour lipstick that gave her face a yellow tinge, that under the pallor her cheeks were round with health. His mother only got tired, not sick like Jude's mother.

Across the way, Eric was dozing and his snores rippled through the room with an unusual, soothing softness. So soothing that Nick found himself telling Maree about Jude, about singing and not singing, about the olive farm and abandoned fires. There were questions, which even in his reverie he knew were unanswerable, so instead he sang her some lines of the song he'd begun for Jude, *I got a heart like an empty glove/ever since you pulled the plug/on the oxygen of your love.* She pretended not to hear the corniness, congratulated him on his biting wit, and he remembered that the peppery scent he'd smelled earlier was of the marigolds he'd once brought Jude. He told his mother nearly, but not quite, everything. Through drooping eyelids Nick watched her listening to him from the visitor's chair, with her face slightly averted to spare him the embarrassment of unburdening. He felt her holding the tip of his finger and he gauged her reactions to what he said when she gripped a little too tightly. He talked softly and, from time to time, Eric's snore punctuated a pause.

Nick woke to faint strums of music. Over on Al's chair, a man was bent over a guitar. Behind him, Lindy, whose eyes were more heavily Cleopatrafied than usual, was hoeing into a bag of peanuts. All Nick could see of the guy was a mess of coarse bleached hair hanging over the guitar. Lindy stooped to hold a handful of peanuts in front of his face, which put him off his tenuous grip on the tune he was working up. It had to be Mark.

'Quit it!' His voice had a nasally, petulant twang, which could have been due to a cold or petulance. Peanuts scattered over the floor as he brushed Lindy's hand away. Nick waited for her reaction. Something about the guy, he didn't know what, made him his natural enemy. He was so wrapped up in himself, maybe that was it.

'Sorry, Marky,' Lindy gushed, disappointing Nick with her submissiveness. She swept aside nuts with her shoes, clearing an exit path as Mark gave the guitar a final irritated strum, then stomped out, his gaze somewhere between his navel and Jupiter. Lindy gaped after him with glowing eyes.

'Al missed you at lunch.' Nick's tone was sharp with accusation against her, for neglecting her routine, the daily observances that kept Al alive and Nick oriented, or at least sane.

'I was waiting for Mark – he's rehearsing for Al's party. It's Al's birthday in a couple of weeks. He'll be thirty-nine.'

Nick whistled. 'That's pretty old.'

'Yes. And I'm twenty-eight.' She raised her eyebrows, waiting.

'What?' he said. 'Oh, I'm nineteen.'

'Ooh.' She drew the word out, as if an awful lot had just been explained. 'Mark's twenty-eight, too.'

'He seems a lot younger,' Nick said, trying out a neutral tone.

'Yes, because he's a surfie,' she said reverentially. 'He went under a wave one day and when he came up he was another Mark. That's the one who's here now, the one I like.'

'How do you know?'

'He told me. I've seen pictures of him – in Surfers.' She sat down stretching her legs out and examining her feet. 'With a surfboard.'

'I mean, how do you know this version of him is the best?'

Lindy eyed him as if he were silly. 'It's all there is.'

Nick nodded. 'He still looks like a surfie.'

Lindy beamed. 'Do you think so?' she gasped. 'That's because of his hair. I do it for him. I never use shampoo and I put salt in to stiffen it, just like a surfie's.' She tried to reach a finger to her callused heel, but her bulk wouldn't let her stretch that far. 'I think I've lost feeling down there.'

'No kidding,' he murmured.

'There aren't any surfies here,' she went on. 'The coast is days away. I went to a beach once, when my parents took one of their holidays from me – they're old and get tired easily and I was a bit of a shock to them. They sent me to one of those homes in Sydney. Some kind of orphanage, I think. It was on the coast, and I liked to look at the sea. Sometimes they'd take us to the lookout, and I could see how big it was and how it moved – you know, kind of gulping. But I didn't like the beach. There was always sand in my socks and the other kids kept trying to jump on me or roll me over and they sent me home when one of the kids got his foot crushed. I didn't like it much. So now my parents send me here when they go away.'

'So you're just here to give your folks a break?' Nick pictured her parents, two elderly, withered people gaping up at Lindy with dismayed reverence – the way he did.

'Well, yes,' she said, fixing him with a tolerant smile. 'It's not like I'm crazy. Hardly anybody here's *crazy* – we just have episodes, some of us. Sunni's the only one who's crazy. But she's about to hook up with one of the Laing boys so that explains it.'

Nick could only nod in agreement because Lindy seemed to know what she was talking about. 'How come you knew my parents were away?'

'I was there when you came in.' When she opened her purse, Nick expected her to produce more peanuts, but she took out a nailfile and began pushing down her cuticles. 'You were lying.'

'The nurses didn't think so – they didn't ship me home.'

'They couldn't tell,' she said. 'You were good at it.'

'But you could tell?'

'It's what I'm best at. It's my vocation.' She laughed, and her laughter – just little breaths really – made her entire body ripple. 'And the nurses wouldn't expect deliberate lies from somebody who was raving like you were.' She leaned towards him, pointing the nailfile to the ceiling, which Nick now thought of as Al's realm. 'But I didn't snitch on you, did I? Keeping secrets is my other vocation.'

'I'll tell you another secret then,' Nick said. 'Mark can't play the guitar.'

'That's not a secret,' she said, rising with slow, icy dignity. 'And it's not the point.' Her soft delivery was like a kick in the head.

'Did I deserve that?' Nick asked Eric when she'd left.

'Yup. You've got a real talent for putting your foot in it.'

'Just when I thought I was getting somewhere.'

Eric guffawed. 'It's a long way before *you* start getting anywhere.'

'Breathe in,' said Beryl. She was the physiotherapist and she'd come to rescue Nick from pneumonia by making him cough his heart out. 'Breathe out.' She'd already saved Eric, who'd coughed all over her effortlessly, and then she'd tackled Al, pulling the sheet from over his head and forcing his curled up body into an exclamation mark. Now she tugged at Nick's toe in what he supposed was an attempt at friendliness before packing the pillows higher behind his back, and pounding him into the proper breathing position. It was not a labour of love, like breathing for a singing lesson, it was a duty to the body.

'In again. Out.' Beryl ignored his resistance and forced him to breathe. Beryl knew how to terrorise: 'If you don't do this, you'll get pneumonia and drown.' She grabbed him by the ankle of his intact leg, twisting it around and back like a lump of pizza dough, bending the knee, making him do it himself until he was about to take a deep breath voluntarily and scream at her, only she wouldn't have heard because her professional patter wiped out all forms of resistance.

'Lift your bottom off the bed. Rotate your shoulders, you've got to keep moving, prevent clots from forming, keep those muscles strong.' With the grip of a fox-trap she rotated his shoulders and this time he did let out a croak, which she ignored. 'Lift your bottom again, dear.' Beryl smiled with satisfaction at his clenched teeth, as if all the energy Nick expended had come from her. 'That's it, keep lifting, do it whenever you think of it, and keep up the breathing.'

'Okay, I'll breathe.'

She left his body alone at last and marched to the door, still blathering. 'Ask the nurses to give your bottom a good rub, dear, it's very red and you don't want to end up with a bedsore, do you?'

No, he wouldn't want to be distracted by a bedsore while he fantasised about women and dogs who were never faithless, or daydreamed that Eric never rattled his bed, nor cleared his clogged throat as he geared up for a talk. He wouldn't want to be distracted by a sore bottom while he pondered the unfairness of the constant gush of his next-bed neighbour Eric, and the realisation that Jude had been drip-feeding him information at a rate she'd thought he could process, and not, as she'd said, because she wanted to prolong the *normality* of their relationship. He had a laugh like fresh water, she'd said, and she didn't want to lose it too soon. No, it was all a lie. He really was that immature, just another urban rube. *I don't want to be happy, I want to be with you*, he'd said. And now, despising himself for knowing there was a song in there he could work up, too guilty to use it.

Two sets of footsteps came down the corridor. One set was Nurse Sunni, carrying the shaving tray. The other was Dave Bear-claw, in black boots.

'Crazy shoes,' Nick said. He'd said that line to himself so many times it had become a refrain. Dave smiled his guileless smile, and the relief on Nurse Sunni's face was insulting.

'A friend!' She gave him the gear. 'Please, you do the honours.'

'Man, I'm sorry about your accident,' Dave said, picking up the razor, and goggling at the brush.

'Not your fault,' Nick said, switching his gaze from Nurse Sunni to Dave's quivering hand. *It was all your fault, you soft-brained knucklehead. It was your dorky white shoes that put me here. It was Robbie's fault too.* 'Did the shoes work?'

Dave looked confused.

'Did you get the girl?'

Dave managed a weak grin. 'Nope.'

'Stick with black, mate. Black boots are always a better bet than white winklepickers.'

Heels clicking to attention, Dave turned to the tray and gingerly picked up the shaving brush. Neck furniture swinging, he craned forward and soaped up Nick's face. Dave's shave was one of atonement. Nick closed his eyes and tried to think of Roy.

Sometime later he woke in a panic. The shaving tray was there, but Dave had gone. He had an erection, must have been dreaming about Jude. It was wearying; these days, he was in a permanent state of extremities – high anxiety when he woke with an erection, terror when he didn't. A new nurse scurried past the doorway, so he called for a bottle. When she came back with it she picked up the skin of his dick as if her fingers were a pair of tongs. *No, don't just plop it in, hold it a little longer, it gets so bedsore*. But she pulled the sheet up to his chest and left him, forgetting to draw the curtain round the bed.

By the time Robbie arrived Nick had joined Al in his search for ceiling cracks. Robbie loped up to the bed, his nails and ears scrubbed shiny pink after a day's picking, and shamelessly unperturbed by the bottle beneath the sheet. Nick tried giving him the silent treatment he'd picked up from Al. But the way Robbie knew just how high to lift the sheet, and just how carelessly to whisk the bottle away and under the bed to save Nick's pride provoked a rush of jealousy that made him break his silence.

'You're the first person to sit there,' he said.

'Your own fault, mate.' Robbie pulled a small stack of CDs from his backpack and stood while he checked through them. 'Maybe you should cut the secret act and let your folks know you're here. And by the way, you could have let me know that was the story – it was a nurse who told me.'

'What? Me call you?' he said looking pointedly at his hands. His eyes slid to Eric and back to Robbie. 'And keep your voice down,' he hissed, then added, 'Don't tell them – Maree will freak.'

'Why not? You've only had an accident.'

'I can't explain things to them. Not yet.'

'Ah.' Robbie slowly nodded his head, grimacing at the plaster on Nick's hands, reminding Nick of how lame he must look in his hospital gown. 'I brought you a talking book and a couple of real ones, but I guess they're not much use if you can't hold them.'

'Leave them, Lindy or Trace might read them to me.'

'So you do have visitors,' Robbie said with undisguised relief.

'Didn't you notice?' He lifted his chin for inspection. 'I've just had a Dave shave.' He nodded towards Al. 'Lindy and Trace are his visitors. They live here.' Robbie wasn't listening; he was eyeing the new nurse who'd come back to collect Nick's bottle. Nick observed his smile at work, making her cheeks blush and turning her eyes all soft and milky as she retreated with Nick's piss. A smile for every occasion, a sneer for every situation.

'Anything else you need?' Robbie said when the nurse had gone.

Yes, call Jude and ask why she hasn't come to see me. Tell her it doesn't matter as long as she pretends to be happy I'm still alive. He took a deep breath, the way Beryl had shown him. 'Yes. You'll have to email Maree. You'll have to pose as me.'

Robbie was silent, moving the shaving tray to make room for the CDs. He stacked them, sat down, and faced Nick. 'No.'

'Just do it once,' Nick pleaded. 'Be me, and tell them I'm going into the wilds for a few weeks picking cotton or something – you know how to say it like me, you're good at that. Please,' he said when Robbie's face remained doubtful. 'Get me over this hump, and I'll sort it out later.'

'Sort it . . . You know how bad I'll look when it all goes skew-whiff?'

Nick nodded.

'Okay, I'll do it once.'

'Thanks mate.' Nick took another deep breath before the

next question. 'How much did you know about Jude?'

Robbie leaned back in the chair, crossed his legs and uncrossed them. 'You mean her inheritance? Max told me. But whatever happened back there with you and her,' he added quickly, 'Jude didn't say and I don't want to know. It's better that way.'

Nick looked at him sharply. You didn't help one bit, he wanted to say, but held his tongue. Robbie was helping now.

The doorway was darkened by the arrival of Lindy, demanding her whip.

Robbie clutched the sides of the chair and stared in awe as she entered the room. Nick smiled; he was beginning to admire the way Lindy moved. He didn't know how she did it with her short skirt, her mighty feet and flimsy stilettos, but she didn't walk so much as proceed like the prow of a ship. She was monumental.

'She's a freak.'

The contempt in Robbie's hushed voice was a shock. A pang of loyalty nipped Nick and he didn't know for whom. But then Robbie sat back with his easy laugh, and Nick decided he'd been imagining things.

Lindy paused to examine Robbie, taking in his lean body, muscled from working the fields, his sleepy blue eyes and his smile that was not directed towards her. She sniffed and moved on.

'Call your folks,' Robbie told Nick. He followed Lindy with wary eyes. 'Get out of here.'

'And be stuck with Maree washing my arse?'

'There's your dad . . . well, there's Bowie . . .' Robbie picked up his backpack and rose, suddenly ready to leave. 'Hire a nurse.'

'I'd rather be here.' He'd rather be back a month ago with Jude, doing it right this time. Nick eyed Robbie, unable to resist a dig. 'Those shoes didn't work for Dave. You gave him bad advice.'

'I never told him to get winklepickers – I wouldn't say that to anybody.'

Lindy had opened Al's locker and taken some chocolates from her stash. She unwrapped two, stuffed them into her mouth, hesitated, then took out another. She seemed to be heading towards Robbie, but then changed her mind and went back to Al. But Robbie had already stepped back, knocking the shaving tray, slopping water everywhere and peppering the CDs with bits of whisker.

'Look out – get a cloth!' Eric ordered him. 'Those discs'll be wet as buggery.'

'Who's that?' Robbie said, mopping around the CDs with Nick's towel, smirking over Eric's bossiness. Nick could have told him, but he realised Robbie didn't really want to know.

'You know what?' Nick said, 'I reckon your life's been as smooth as dairy whip.'

Robbie stopped mopping. 'What's that supposed to mean?'

Nick knew the look he gave him, he knew dozens of Robbie's looks and none of them could match Jude's, none of them were going to intimidate him. But he couldn't bring himself to tell Robbie that Lindy was no freak. That would be crossing the floor.

'I'm saying all your drama comes from books. You're a safe plot with a guaranteed happy ending.'

'So what's the problem?'

'You're so smug, so contented.'

'What did you ever have to complain about until now? If you weren't in here you'd be going along just like me – contented. No, you'd be *aimlessly* contented.' Robbie dropped the wet towel on the floor. 'I'm not going to change just because *you* had an accident.'

Although Nick didn't believe any of it, Robbie's words stung. But he wasn't going to argue, not when he needed Robbie to help him out. The way he coughed his heart out would have made Beryl proud. 'Maybe, I dunno . . .'

Robbie looked at him with suspicion and relief. 'So what're you doing with yourself besides dumping on people?'

'All I'm doing is thinking about the day I'll be able to roll over.'

'That's the way, aim low.'

Now Eric did his cough. 'That table's still dripping,' he said to Robbie. 'Lindy, love, get him another cloth.'

Lindy snatched up Eric's towel, and tossed it to Robbie with a scowl. 'Where's my planet!' she roared.

'Not here,' Robbie muttered. He mopped a bit more, then dropped the towel on the floor with the other one. 'Gotta run, I'm late for a date.'

'Don't forget to email my folks.'

Eric waved him out. 'See you, matey.'

Lindy came over, unwrapping the chocolate Nick supposed was meant for Robbie. For a moment he thought she was going to give it to him, the first she would have offered, but her thick pliant fingers placed it delicately in her own mouth. Chewing carefully – it must have had a caramel centre – she stuffed the wrapper in her purse, as she always did.

'Your friend's not very good with women.'

'He's having a bad hair day.' Nick gave a small embarrassed laugh. Addicted to normal, was more like it. Lindy looked thoughtfully at him, prompting him to add, 'I didn't mean it when I said Mark was a lousy guitarist.'

'That's all right,' she said kindly. 'You're not very good with anybody.'

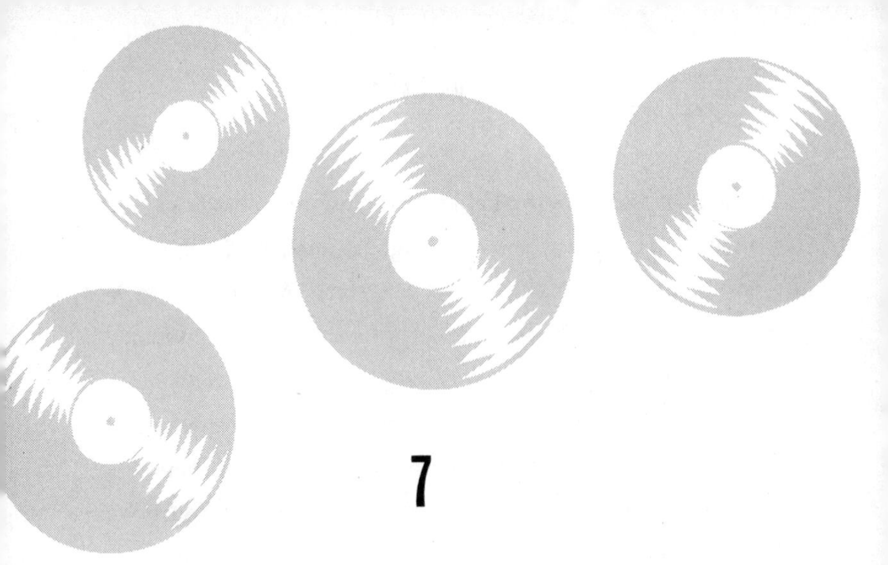

7

AFTER TWO HARD DAYS PICKING TOMATOES, NICK HAD MADE around twenty dollars.

'You gotta pick better – like this.' Tony demonstrated again, his knobby fingers doing exactly what Nick thought he'd been doing, only a lot faster. 'There's a knack.' Tony straightened up with barely a creak and turned to Robbie. 'It's in the hands, the touch. Your dad got a knack for making gelato and I got it for tomatoes.' He held up his square palms. 'We got such good knacks, now we don't have to do it no more, got others doing it for us.'

It was the end of the day and the other pickers were drifting up to the van from the tomatoes. The field stretched flatly, forever, an evermore of rubbery green tomatoes fading into yellow before bouncing back firm and red. With crows floating above in air that boiled his eyes and singed his nostrils, working in the field was as close to hell as Nick could imagine. There was the bending that had him crippled by noon; there were flies, there was thirst, and the deep and fleeting relief of biting into a hot ripe tomato, knowing it would lighten his load and his wages. And then there was the constant sense of futility as he crept down one row and up the next to fill a bottomless box. Robbie did no better, and at this rate they'd both be destitute in a week. 'You got no knack for tomatoes, Roberto,' Tony said sadly. 'Hope you got one for gelato.'

'I'm going to be a gardener, Tony,' said Robbie. 'I'll need the growing knack, not the picking one.'

Taking a tomato from a box, Tony heaved a sigh as he inspected it. He put the fruit back and then gave Nick the same scrutiny. 'And you, Nicko, what's your knack?'

'Nothing in particular,' he answered sheepishly. 'I'm just a general kind of knackless guy.'

Tony grunted in disgust and went to start the van. 'Get in!' he yelled.

Robbie and Nick climbed in with the other pickers, mostly backpackers, and in the confined space of the van the Irish, Danish and German accents formed a chorus. Robbie homed in on the Irish girls, Angie and Enya. Nick was smiling, because even hell could gain a cool blue light if he thought about Jude, and today was Wednesday, the night of her gig. Tony dropped him and Robbie at the shed, and continued with the others to their camp on the edge of town. Nick hobbled up the rough plank steps into the cavernous space, dappled with light trickling through slatted timber walls. Sacks of wheat were stacked in a corner and a row of stretchers lined one wall. The wood floor, smooth, black and shiny with age and footsteps, creaked softly as he limped to his stretcher at one end of the row and fell onto it with exhaustion. Robbie's stretcher was at the other end. The entire picking crew could have lived here, but it was close to Tony's house, and he reserved it for family. There was a single gas burner for cooking, one overhead light, a water tank outside and a stock of mosquito coils that they kept by their stretchers.

While Robbie read bits from a botanical dictionary, a manga comic and *Catch 22*, Nick tracked the golden light as it shifted along the room. It reminded him of sitting in the corner of Cliff's shed, watching shafts of sunlight enter through the greasy windows like ghost fingers daring him to wait for the ghost body to follow. While Cliff tinkered, he'd waited, disappointed and relieved that fingers were all that came. Now the golden fingers were nudging him into an uneasy sleep. He was half-afraid Robbie would let him sleep through Jude's gig, too afraid these last two days to even mention her.

When he woke, Robbie was ambling towards him in pink sneakers and a Hawaiian shirt. Nick shaded his eyes against the dazzle. 'You brought that stuff with you?'

'They're rockabilly party clothes – wherever you go, there'll be a party or rockabilly.'

Nearly Jude time. Nick's legs recovered their spring. He leapt from the stretcher and dashed outside to wash and dress. When he came back Robbie flicked a disdainful, scrubbed finger at his T-shirt. 'And you look so . . . ordinary.'

'You're the one who said "when in doubt wear black".'

'What've you got to be doubtful about?'

He looked deliberately at Robbie. 'Nothing.'

𝄞

As soon as they parked the Toyota they could hear the twangs of guitars coming through the walls of The Fat Stag, and weaving between the guitars was a woman singing them across the car park. It might have been a rockabilly song, but it was a siren's voice and it was reeling him in. By the time they got in the door the voice had landed him. Jude's last note was hanging in the smoky air. Then she left the stage and headed to the Ladies. He gaped in disbelief.

'We're early, how'd we miss her?'

'Settle down,' Robbie said, looking around the nearly deserted bar. 'Nothing's started yet.' He went to get drinks and came back with a Coke for Nick. A couple of guys dressed just like Robbie were lounging against the wall; Robbie joined them while Nick took himself and his feeble drink to the bar. It wasn't only because he couldn't afford it that he didn't drink alcohol. He didn't have the taste for it yet. One day it would arrive, but until then he preferred his drinks sweet. He was good at shamming, he thought, watching Jude head his way. Nobody would mistake him for a wimp, he thought, ditching the pink straw Robbie had deliberately left in the glass. 'I missed your song,' he said to her.

'No you didn't, it was a sound-check,' she said, greeting him with a touch on his arm. 'It was just a lot of humming.' Her voice wrapped round him like a velvet shawl, slipping off when she turned to take the beer the barman handed her. A few old blokes leaned against their own bit of bar, providing the smoky accompaniment for the air. Over by the wall Robbie and his look-alike guys were gabbing like old buddies.

'The show starts soon,' said Jude, waving to Robbie and the guys. 'But Stu's going to rehearse a number first.' She gestured at the nonexistent crowd. 'It'll be a kind of private welcome-to-Crundle show for you and Robbie.' Just then, as if he'd heard his name, Robbie sent her an affectionate smile, and Jude returned it. 'He was good fun when we were ten,' she said. 'A little bit dangerous.'

'Still is,' Nick said dryly, trying not to sound jealous. 'A natural-born operator with a mercury smile. Did you really sing him Mongolian folk songs?'

'No, that's just Robbie – you know Robbie.' Her conspiratorial smile was so fleeting Nick almost missed it: we know Robbie. 'But my mother probably sang them,' she went on. 'She must have known just about every song in the world – she got them from our olive pickers. Back then, I would've known Greek, Hungarian, Gipsy, Italian songs.' She drained her beer and put it on the bar. 'Even Australian ones.'

Down where the band was loosely arranged on a makeshift stage, the double-bass player was talking to his instrument while he tuned the fat strings. 'That's Steve,' said Jude. 'He holds us all together.'

'Stu!' Steve called. 'You want to get up here?' One of Robbie's buddies pulled himself away from the wall and loped down to the band. He mumbled something, counted in the beat with his foot and burst into 'Blue Suede Shoes'. Nick felt his mouth slipping into a smirk at the predictable choice when he suddenly heard something. There was a vibrato, a catch in the phrasing that made him listen. He watched Jude listen while she contemplated her hands, her shoulders twitching in time with the snare drum.

'He's getting better,' she said.

The crowd started arriving, pulling Jude into its circulation. Most were dressed for the occasion, girls in pedal pushers, pointy flat shoes and high ponytails; all the guys looked like they'd gone to the same barber for their ducktails and flat-tops, and bought their fluorescent-lime and baby-blue shirts at the same shop as Robbie. It was like a club, Nick thought, and the backpacker pickers, blue-eyed and red-haired, served as a counterpoint. Only Jude, moving through the flamboyant crowd, seemed an outsider in her old jeans, boots and skimpy singlet. He ordered drinks and took Robbie his beer. 'Nobody looks like this in Sydney,' he said. 'Except you.'

'Sure they do, you just don't go to the right places.'

A guy was standing in front of him at the bar with a bunch of pink daisies tattooed up the side of his neck and a hairdo you could dive from. He turned, exposing a hefty brass belt buckle and a face ravaged with pockmarks and creases. The daisies only made him menacing and Nick had a vision of him in Time Warp, the gun-runner's offsider. The guy raised his beer, flashing a ring of silver and turquoise set around a mud-coloured stone.

'What's that, mate?' Nick nodded at the stone which was almost as long as the guy's pinkie.

'Bear's claw,' the guy said proudly. He flashed a smaller version of the ring on his other hand. 'And that's a baby bear's claw.'

'Die of old age, did they?' Robbie asked, coming up for another beer.

Doubt crumpled the guy's face. 'Nobody said they were dead. Bloke told me they were nail clippings.'

'Leave it, Robbie,' Nick muttered. 'You'll have him bawling.'

'Only kidding, mate,' Robbie said, slapping him on the shoulder. The guy moved off, easing his way between three women, cracking a joke with them, the way you do when you know three good-looking women well, Nick thought, though he didn't know any women like that. He finished his Coke and turned to watch the hairdos dance, wondering where Jude was. The band kept playing, Stu sang another song, and the Irish girls, Angie and Enya, broke into a jig that perfectly suited the rockabilly rhythm. Other singers came up to take Stu's place, some of them dazzlingly bad, and everyone loved them and applauded even louder. Nick joined the backpackers, trying to be cool, pretending his eyes weren't trailing after Jude. Most people knew her, yet there was a reserve in their manner that wasn't simply due to the unconforming clothes she wore. Jude didn't seem to notice, or else she took it as her due. At last she completed the circuit and was back to him.

'I'm up next,' she said, glancing down at her hands. 'I'm doing my own song.'

'*Your* song?' breathed Nick.

'You wrote it?' Robbie asked.

She nodded. 'But it's just a tune.'

There was uncertainty in her voice, yet she strolled down to the band and took the mike as if she were entering her own kitchen sink for a glass of water. She was better at shamming than Nick was. Steve led in and the guitarists started strumming. Treating the mike like a lover's ear, her voice was effortless. All that humming she'd done earlier, so that now it seemed she didn't have to breathe. Her hands were still except for a finger now and then etching something on the air. Her song was about losing somebody and no hope of getting them back and the chorus kept returning to the word 'underground'. It wasn't quite rockabilly, and sounded personal when she sang *underground ain't where you belong*. But sounding personal was what singing was about, so maybe she hadn't lost the love of her life; maybe she was just good at writing those kinds of songs.

When her set was over she joined the other singers by the wall. That must be what happened when a bunch of singers got together; it was a club and it didn't matter if you were a cowboy or a baker, he thought, wondering what she did for a living.

Robbie was being attentive to Irish Angie, who was showing him a jig step. Nick eased his way through the crowd, and outside for air and nearly tripped over the sleeping dogs tied to the corner post. One yelped, the other growled, but he hardly noticed, because Jude was suddenly there, untying them, soothing them.

'Nice dogs,' he said. 'What are they, baby greyhounds?'

'Whippets.' She pointed to one. 'That's Biff, and this is Boof.'

'How can you tell them apart?' The quick sympathetic

smile she gave him made him sorry he'd asked. 'I meant it'd be hard for me – not knowing them.' He wasn't crazy about dogs. Lois, the family spaniel, was tolerable because Cliff looked after her, and she was more like a senile great-aunt than a dog. And Bowie's puppy would be entirely Bowie's. These two were suss, too much like what things called whippets should look like – too smart, too attached to Jude, too much in his way. He could see them sensing competition too.

'Did you find many ticks the other night? My dog Lois never gets them – one of the perks of living in the city.' He rushed on, praying – *just don't show yourself up for the fool you are* – 'Your song was fantastic and I love your voice, it's so . . . unusual.'

They stared at each other, Nick cursing himself. All those books Robbie had foisted onto him, all those useful words – gone. 'You've got great control,' he finally said.

She gave a strangled kind of giggle. 'Do you sing?'

'I used to want to – you know, teenage fantasy stuff.' He knew that the corners of his mouth betrayed his uncertainty, that his eyes were almost crossed with intensity. He could feel her reading him, the hope, the yearning for experience, for the meaning that might come of it. The list might as well be stapled to his brow. 'I used to want to sing like Roy Orbison.'

She glanced down the hill, then back to him, sympathetic. 'He's hard, all right.'

'I used to hear him in my dad's shed.'

She listened as if she knew already, as if his memory was shared. And there he was again, a kid on Saturday mornings, hanging about outside Cliff's shed, waiting for him to finish tinkering with his ancient telephones, waiting for him to come outside to play. The radio resonating against the tin walls while Roy cried for Leila, making loneliness bite so hard he'd expected to see blood.

'I wanted to break hearts like Roy.' He laughed and shrugged, stealing a peek at her, thinking about her hair and how having it tied back with the bandanna was a little old-fashioned, and thinking how much he wanted to bury his face in it. 'I pushed it down when computer games and cars came along.' He shrugged again. 'It's still there, but it only rises in dreams. And I probably need more heartache to sing like Roy.'

'You'd need his voice too. But you're the dark brooding type, it'll come,' she said in her mock Gothic tone, looking back down the hill. 'Grief and heartache, that is.'

'If anyone's going to give me grief, it'll be my kid-brother.' He babbled on, because she was no effort to be with, to talk to, hunkered down by the dogs with her hands hanging between her knees and her mouth twitching at Bowie's name. 'It's spelt Beau,' he explained. 'And he just needs a bit of steering home.'

Then she was gone. The thing she'd been looking for, a black Rodeo, rumbled up the hill and did a U-turn. The door swung open, the dogs jumped in and Jude followed them.

'Next week!' she yelled from the window as the ute took off down the hill. Nick waved, wondering who the man in the hat behind the wheel was.

Back inside, Robbie and Angie had been joined by more backpackers. Another singer had joined the band. This guy's nasal twang was too thin to fill the room or compete with the guitar, but in his stovepipe pants and tasselled red fez he was spiffy in an other-world, other-time kind of way, and Nick liked the way he closed his eyes on the right note and hunched over with a sax-player-curve to his spine. It didn't matter that his voice was thin because it had feeling, and he looked like a singer, looked like he knew what he was doing. The bear-claw guy was out there with a ponytailed girl in green pedal pushers. They rocked and jived, he with his brass buckle providing pelvic thrust, and flashing a hopeful smile at the girl, who flashed hers on the singer in the fez.

Rockabilly music was nothing serious, nothing to fall in love with. 'But it's fun,' he said to Robbie when he joined Nick at the bar. 'It's got a beat that starts in your balls and never tries to get any higher.'

They hung around watching the scene for a while, and eventually saw the singer with the fez leave with the girl in the green pedal pushers.

'Didn't see him look at her once,' Robbie said admiringly as they walked to the car. Nick was taken aback by a hot-dog man who had set up at the entrance to the car park. 'Hiya,

Toby,' Robbie said to him. 'Toby's the butcher,' he told Nick.

Standing further along, with a sausage in his fist and dejection on his face, was the bear-claw guy. Nick nodded as they passed him. 'I bet he didn't see the singer look at her, either,' he said.

'That Angie's all right,' Nick said casually, as they drove away. 'She can dance. Pretty, too.'

'She's nice.' Robbie's voice was neutral.

8

NURSE SUNNI MOVED TO A HOSPITAL RHYTHM. HER HIPS didn't sway to slide guitars or drum rolls. No undulating sax or slithering clarinet, Nurse Sunni's walk clipped along to the ting of bells and trolley wheels, the wheeze of resuscitation machines, the swing of drip tubes and the thump of bed boards. The walls stood to attention when Nurse Sunni passed. She was taking Nick down on his own tinging trolley to the bowels where Nuke Med lived and where Eric had said there were three witches who controlled it, waiting behind lead shields with their zap guns. She was taking him down to see if his wrist bones were still alive.

'You won't be radioactive when you come out,' Nurse Sunni informed him. 'It's only a CAT scan to make sure your wrists haven't succumbed to necrosis of the bone tissue.'

'So necrosis is some kind of eczema, is it?' he asked her, feeling a sudden need to urinate.

'No. It's death of the bone tissue.' She lined him up alongside another trolley in the waiting area. 'An orderly will bring you back when it's over,' she said before abandoning him.

'What're you having?' A balding woman lay on the trolley beside him, so skeletal he'd dismissed her for a rumple in the blanket.

'CAT scan.'

The woman sniffed. 'That's a doddle, it's just diagnostic. It's not *treatment*.'

It was probably the done thing to ask what her treatment was, but she sounded like she'd sampled them all, and he didn't want to know. When somebody, maybe one of the witches, came to get him, he was almost relieved.

'This is a painless procedure, Mr Green.'

They'd removed the plaster for the duration of the scan, and he steeled himself for a quick peep at his arms and hands. They were wasted. Fascinated by the maggoty whiteness of his wrists and fingers, he couldn't shift his eyes. They were somebody else's hands. It was only temporary, he told himself; they'd wrap him up again when the scan was over, and at the next unveiling he'd be recovered, a new Nick emerging from under the plaster, like surfie Mark from his wave.

Everything was ready to go. The head witch had retreated behind her shield and was about to press the button that would send Nick sliding into the tunnel. He'd have twenty uninterruptible minutes to lie in it and maybe sort out his life.

'What was that, Mr Green?' The witch spoke with a withering patience.

'I need the bottle.'

'Try to hold on, we'll be finished soon.'

'I don't think I can hold on.'

'Bring the boy a bottle,' she hissed at her underling.

Too late.

Don't think about Jude, and you can bear anything. Think about her and you can bear even more – but not the piss that burned down your leg.

They cleaned him up and sent him back into the tunnel.

The bald woman was still there when they brought him back to the waiting area for pickup. Waiting must have been part of her treatment.

'How'd you go?' she asked.

'I got put into a steel drum and rotated at a slow burn,' he said, watching a stream of water head their way along the floor.

'Oh yes, the suckling pig.' It was probably only her illness that made her skin green, but her smile was ghoulish.

'It'll be raining upstairs,' she said as the stream washed by them. 'This is always the first place to flood. Hullo, Trace, dear.'

Nick started. He couldn't see because he was facing the wrong way, but there was no mistaking Trace's chirpy delivery. 'Hi Nick, hullo Mrs B. All right?' And her raucous smoker's laugh when Mrs B said, 'Ready to die, but who'll look after my hydrangeas, then?'

'Nice and blue are they?'

'Blue as misery, Trace, thank you. How's Lindy?'

'Still a goer, that Lindy.'

Who were these people? Talking like they lived here. Lindy and her flock of gossips and protégés, organising a party for a guy near zombiedom. Sometimes he didn't believe that Lindy and Trace's ward existed. There was another community here, operating between the floors, probably between the walls. And that'd be the water supply, he decided, listening to the floor slurping with run-off.

The head witch's underling came out and wheeled Mrs B away. Then Trace was standing beside him, holding her slippers.

'What are you doing here?' Nick asked.

'Mark's down there.' She pointed her chin towards the dark recesses of the corridor. 'He and Lindy had one of their fights and she told him he couldn't play guitar for peanuts.'

Don't ask, Nick told himself, she'll think you're nosy – worse, she'll think you're interested.

'What are they fighting about?'

Trace's sparse eyebrows were raised with surprise. 'Don't you know? He caught a bus to the coast last week with Jilly Jackson. She's a hairdresser.' The last word was uttered in an undertone with a grimace that Nick took to be sympathy for Lindy. He was grimacing back when she said, 'Have they forgotten you again?'

'No,' he said, a bit offended at her bluntness. 'Somebody's on their way.'

'Well!' she said, 'I'll just wait with you awhile.'

'What about Mark?'

'I'm early,' she whispered, darting a look down the corridor. 'He won't be expecting me for a few minutes.' Trace was a bird, a scrawny sparrow, flitting around, pecking away at Nick's defences with the confiding tone of her chatter. 'We're all local. We know Bert's wife and Mrs B – she was our science teacher. We know Eric and Iris and we used to know their son Joe.'

'Is that what Eric looks at in Iris's bag? A picture of his son?'

'Yes.'

'What happened to him?'

Trace pulled back a little. 'You'll have to ask him.'

'How long have you been coming here, Trace?'

'Years, hon.'

'Did you know Leni Brack?'

'We saw her,' Trace said, frowning. 'We didn't know her.'

Nick raised his head as far as he could, his voice rising. 'Did you know her daughter?'

'She was just a little girl.' Trace hugged her slippers to her chest, closing down in the face of Nick's helpless tone. His head slumped back onto the pillow. He was hungry for more, but there was nothing she would tell him. He was grateful for the time wrinkle, that Trace had seen Jude as a little girl. He didn't find it strange that Trace remembered her; she wasn't somebody you'd forget.

'Trace?'

'Hmm?' The water had subsided, and she was putting her slippers on.

'I'm sorry I went off at you that time.'

'I know that, hon.'

He watched her make her way down the corridor, to the other-world. How Trace managed to dart about in her clumsy bumblebee slippers was another of life's unsolved mysteries.

He called out to her again. 'Why do you wear those slippers?'

'For ballast!' Extending her arms, she turned full circle in little hops. Then she came back to him. 'She was just a girl, and we saw her grow up. She came for eight years and she'd sit with her mum and sing to her and most of the time her mum forgot who she was. She has bad associations with this place, same as Al. So don't be mad at her if she doesn't come to see you.'

She wouldn't come anyway; she was further off into the wilds than he'd ever go, singing every song as if it were her last.

That night he dreamed he was trying to wake up. Trying, but the microphone was one of those creamed tapioca types and kept dripping down his hand. Caught in a dream and because it was a dream he was on a stage. His joints had seized as usual and he'd forgotten the words to the song. His leaden feet had dropped anchor at the bottom of the harbour, and in the blinding spotlight he watched the audience like a patient watching a doctor read their test results. The doctor took pity and whacked one of his feet free with a baton.

Nick's shriek woke him and he blinked in the sudden moonlight. Al was at the end of his bed, plucking at Nick's big toe. It was the toe attached to his unbroken leg, glowing white in the moonlight, paler than Al's fingers. Did he think it was uncontaminated food, Nick wondered. He tried to withdraw his foot, but Al had a grip on it. They stared at one another, Al with his glazed white skin and his coal-pit eyes. Nick looked into his eyes and it was like standing on the edge of an abyss. He recognised it, an unfathomable, despairing, sorrow, the place where Al's silence lived. He'd seen something like it before, not in Jude, but in her father, Bruno.

'I hope somebody loves you, Al.' Al's knees groaned as he sank onto them, pulling Nick's leg down with him. His other leg stayed anchored to its pulley making him half spread-eagled. Al laboured for breath, struggling to move along with Nick's toe. He didn't know where Al intended heading, but he was too weak to make much progress. Nick thought of all the food that never made it to Al's mouth. Without the tiny morsels Lindy got into him, he'd be dead by now. Only Lindy loved him.

'Nurse!' Nick yelled. He could have kicked himself free, but he didn't do things like that anymore and he didn't want to frighten Al.

'Get into bed, Joe, or I'll shoot you,' Eric intoned groggily.

'What the hell are you saying?' Nick snapped, waking Eric fully. 'I'll shoot you!'

'Mr Green!' the nurse cried, flicking on the light as she rushed in. Glowering at Nick as she unwound Al's fingers from his toe, she said, 'Threats against other patients will not be tolerated.' She hoicked Nick's leg back onto the bed then tried to heave Al up to his feet, but he clung to the floor. She called for another nurse.

'By jingo, it's a busy place,' said Eric when nobody came to help. 'Full moon, probably. You might have to sit on him,' he advised the nurse when Al started his slow crawl again. 'And it's back to the Gulag for you, my lad,' he added to Nick, 'threatening to shoot people.'

'You're a frigging agitator – and he's Al, not Joe,' Nick began, but stopped to watch a big male nurse sweep in and pick up Al as if he were a stick insect.

'Get into bed, Al,' the guy boomed heartily, 'or I'll give you an injection.' This time the threat worked.

'Where *were* you?' the other nurse muttered.

'Busy night,' the guy said. 'Full moon.'

'You've got to take him back – he doesn't even belong in the renal ward, let alone here.'

'Can't.' He dropped Al on the bed and shrugged. 'We're full.'

They bedded Al down and gave him an injection anyway. The room filled with its foul smell as the nurses headed for the door. Nick called to them. The female nurse stopped and turned.

'What was that, Mr Green?'

'I said you should get Lindy,' Nick said. 'He didn't just want a bite of my toe. He's sick.' What kind of sickness, he had no idea.

'We know he's ill, but Lindy's not going to cure him.'

'She'd cure him before you lot would,' Nick retorted.

The nurse sighed. 'There is no cure, Mr Green, only treatment.' She switched off the light and left.

Eric's voice came through the dark. 'Good lad.'

'What did Al want?'

'To go away, I suppose,' Eric said. 'Like the rest of us, only a lot more and a lot further.'

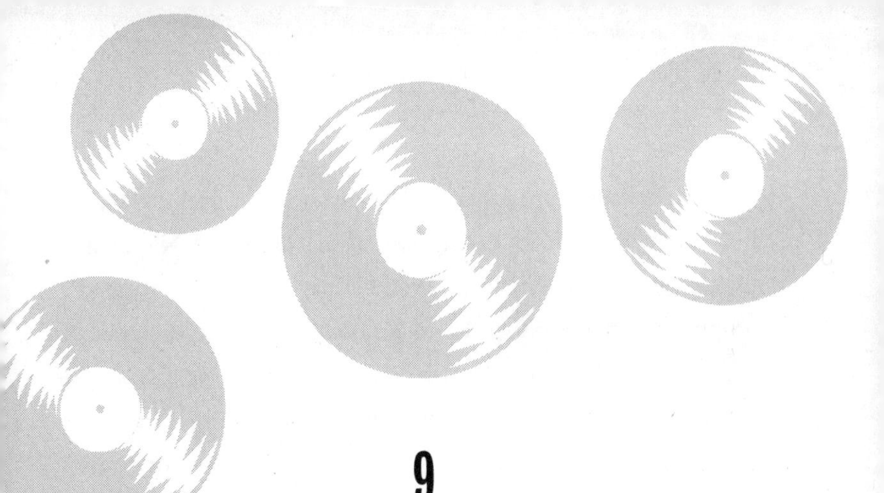

9

'I'VE NEVER SEEN AN OLIVE TREE.'

It was Wednesday night again. Hours before, Nick had arrived with Robbie and left him prattling with the bear-claw guy. He'd set himself up at the stage end of the bar, to be close when Jude arrived.

From the back wall came the cheery ring and zing and lights of the two poker machines, but the rest of the place was dim, with its smoke-stained walls and steep ceiling, the only evidence of its former life as a church. It was like sitting in an old brown photograph, but Nick loved it because it was Jude's pub. A stream of cowboy hats had meandered through the door and they trickled quietly into the grungy backpacker crowd when the music began.

The band was tight, but the voice was wrong. Some woman who wasn't Jude was singing. She was pretty, she had the movements, the patter and she could sing. The slow country ballads slipped around the room like a friendly arm, but country wasn't rockabilly; she wasn't Jude, and Nick was drifting. He hung his head over his flat Coke, and clapped limply after her number. He was about to ask the bartender where Jude was when the singer introduced 'Our Next Guest'.

Jude appeared from the direction of the women's toilets and made her entrance. She walked up to the microphone, wrapping her fingers round it as if it were just another person she'd found to chew the fat with. He never used to pay much attention to what girls wore, only what bits of body they emphasised or left bare. Now he noticed the red fringe on her short black skirt and her red cowboy boots. They didn't leave all that much exposed, and he couldn't pinpoint what was special about her, but she made him ache in the right places. Simple. She looked like a baton-twirling cowgirl at a rodeo, and that was fine because now she was singing a cowgirl song, *no branding iron gonna make me yours*, using the hum of the crowd as another layer of sound to play with. Okey dokey, Nick thought, I'll love her music, even if it does swing by the prairie.

She was fooling a swirling ballad into doing things it shouldn't be able to do when a guy, with pouches under his eyes and a sixties cop-show hat Nick recognised as the one in the black ute, moved in and sat between Nick and the stage. As Jude finished the song and opened her eyes she focused on the hat guy straight away. Her spot was over and so was the set. Nick's applause drowned everyone else's. The other singer, who'd been sitting to the side, took the microphone. 'Thanks for upstaging me, Jude,' she said with a laugh at Nick.

The Hat followed Jude to the bar. All Nick had to do was walk up, put himself next to the Hat and hope she'd choose to see him. Frozen, he thought of all those girls with tongues and eyes like swords that he used to leer at. It was a habit, he supposed, to compare the hilts of legs, the points of breasts. Fixations he'd learned to swing between until somebody came along who stopped him in midair. Now he was turning blue from dangling and he wasn't sure she'd noticed.

They descended on her at the same time. Just as the Hat's hand came to rest on her shoulder Nick butted in. *Speak music to her, the way musos do.*

'You were fantastic,' he blurted. 'The way you use all those . . .' *This is what happens when you don't speak music* '. . . notes.'

The Hat snorted, but Jude flashed Nick a smile.

'Thanks, Nick.'

'They really like you,' he said, nodding at the crowd.

'Yep, I'm the ant's pants for five minutes – but five minutes is better than nothing, eh, Max?' she said, grabbing the guy's arm.

When she dropped it, Nick inhaled again. Maybe he was an ex, or a cousin. 'You left that other singer for dead,' he said.

'No, I didn't,' she said. 'Kaylee's much better, and a pro – but thanks for saying it.'

What she meant was, *If you knew the first thing about singing, you'd know that.* Nick nodded. *Thanks for being kind.*

'Jude . . .' Max began.

Jude had a past; her life hadn't begun when he entered it and he wasn't even really in it yet. Better jump in fast.

'Max, I'm Nick. What kind of hat is that?'

Max scowled at him. 'It's a porkpie. See you in a minute, Jude.'

'An old friend?' he asked as Max walked away.

'An old friend and a neighbour, and he wants to be my manager.'

Nick turned his head to hide whatever was showing on his face, saw Robbie eyeing him from the corner, and turned back. 'Is he any good at it?'

'Don't know yet. He's been trying to line up a little country tour. He's gruff, but it's a pose.' She grimaced. 'Part of the management look.'

'So you are good – it's not just me being a fan.'

Her smile was not coy, nor was it cynical. 'Well, Max has a lot of faith. You listen to somebody you know, they always sound great. Frank and Sue have their fans too,' she said, gesturing towards a couple wearing matching silver shirts and neck scarves. They looked familiar to Nick. 'They own the newsagents and they're famous for being the two worst singers in town.' That was it, he'd sent an email from their shop.

'I'm okay and so are a million others,' Jude said. 'It's just how much you want the singing life.' Her gaze dropped to her boots. 'I want that life,' she said, raising her head. 'I don't want to die selling nails at Shirley's Hardware.'

It was then, not wanting to hear about plans that might involve another guy, that he told her that he'd never seen an olive tree. Her face was radiant as she described what it felt like to sit in the palm of branches that twisted out into black fingers that sprouted cool silvery-grey leaves. 'You climb up into another world. It's like being under some god's umbrella, and the sun can't burn you,' she told him. 'An olive tree is one of the best things in the world – ask Robbie.'

'Um . . . I'd rather just come and see one.'

Together they contemplated his trembling hands. 'I don't have a car – I ride in with Max,' she said.

'I'll get there.'

'It's a long way.'

'I'll make it.'

𝄞

On Saturday afternoon Tony let Nick use one of his grown son's bicycles.

'He's gone to the big smoke, got no use for it,' Tony said glumly, wheeling it out from the garden shed. 'Tyres need some air, that's all.' He handed Nick a chain, a padlock and a helmet. 'You need a helmet. A lotta trucks – they throw up a lotta stones. You need a chain. You never know who's gonna be a thief.'

'You want to ride to Marston?' Robbie said incredulously when Nick rode it back to the shed. 'It won't fit in the Toyota when you keel over and need rescuing.'

'I thought I'd skip Marston and ride down the road a bit, take a look around.'

'Uh huh.' Robbie gave the pumped tyres a desultory kick. 'What direction were you thinking of heading?'

Nick pointed vaguely west. 'I wouldn't want to backtrack.' When Robbie's eyes narrowed, he said quickly, 'You're going to town with Angie, aren't you?'

'Yeah.'

Robbie retreated inside the shed. Nick clipped on the helmet and rode down the track to the road, sailing past crops of capsicums, cucumbers and the relentless tomatoes, past orchards of peach and orange trees. When the river took a turn, he hit the other side of the plain, and realised that Crundle was a renegade green bump in a big brown platter. Shadows were lengthening, cooling the late afternoon, and he'd be able to see a truck coming for miles so he took off the helmet. His head felt light, as exposed as the land that seemed to spread further as he rode through it. The humming of his tyres was absorbed into the blanket of hushed air, the stillness punctured from time to time by buzzing fat bluebottles, or a bored cark from a crow that was dogging him. It was so flat that he barely had to pedal, and he drifted along with his floating thoughts, wishing that in the end they would all add up to something, instead of disappearing into etherland, never to be thought again.

Ride for two hours, she'd said, *and start looking out for me on the roadside*. As the second hour advanced so did his anticipation, excitement and fear. She'd told him she lived with her father on the river bank, that her mother was dead. He scanned the distant thin line of trees where the river wound back on itself, wondering where a girl and her father and an olive grove would fit. But he rode steadily and soon the trees were before him, and the road hugged the perimeter of what seemed a forest of eucalypts.

He heard the dogs first, barking somewhere among the trees. Then they leapt into the road ahead of him, Biff and Boof with their wet gobstopper eyes sprinting up to bite at his wheels.

'Nick!' Jude emerged from the trees, a string bag lumpy with oranges and a water bottle over her shoulder. She waved to him then shouted at the dogs. 'Get back here!' She stood with her fists on her hips while they pussyfooted between her and the wheels of his bike. Devotion won out and they slunk back to her, Nick trailing them.

'You made it,' she said, giving him an orange and a soft kiss close to his mouth that set him trembling.

'It was easy.' He straddled the bike, stumped for words, and peeled the orange while he took in her heavy loose hair and her hand removing the bandanna from round her neck. She offered it to him, and he took it, breathing in its faint scent of eucalyptus as he wiped his face. He went to give it back, but she gently pushed back his hand.

'You'll need it again. We're still a long way from home.'

Now that he'd stopped riding the air was solidifying, compacting into a wall against which cicadas threw their song and through which Jude was leading him. He didn't know how she navigated. Every space between the trees looked like a track to him, but Jude could tell the fakes. They wound between stringy-barks and paperbarks, the only names he knew, though there were others. He grabbed at the peeling shreds. Spongy, flesh-coloured and warm, the bark felt alive. There were so many trees, dangling shanks of low branches, so many other, invisible, things he wanted to reach for and touch. She walked beside him, and sometimes ahead. All the while they were watching each other. There was something about her that was different, but all he could come up with was that her eyes seemed darker out here.

Then there was the river, not ahead of them, but running alongside. He'd heard it earlier, but had thought it must be something about the air, thick with echo. Now he recognised a steady drift of water, smelled its brown smell, and soon they came to a stand of rivergums. He leaned the bike against the dappled red, green and grey trunk of one. The dogs took off into the gloom, down where the water was turning black with the evening. She turned to say something and he was touching her palms, touching her ears, bending to take his breath from the pale back of her neck, and he felt the weighty swing of her hair like a length of chain that he twisted back now. Her eyes, as soft and dark and deep as her smile, said yes.

Once he had dreamed of water, so light and clear, that when he went to plunge his head into it he found he was already beneath the surface. Searching for resistance and finding none, discovering he was under only when he raised his head to see light above the surface. It should be strange, another world, he shouldn't breathe so easily underwater, underJude. As if he should have always been there, escaped from the wrong place, and now arrived where he belonged. Only her black eyes could drown him, and she kept them closed, kept him alive with her blindness. Her ankles, her bruising fingers, her rough knees, all of them urgent. All the fumblings and gropings of past experience, they fell away, and he found the rhythm of the ground they lay on. Jude had let him in.

They walked along the river, Nick wheeling the bike and Jude pulling another leaf from his hair. He'd tried to bury the condom under one of the gums, but she'd taken it from him, emptied it and balled it up. 'We'll have to take it back for the garbage,' she told him. He'd felt like a rube from the city, sullying her territory, but she laughed it off. 'You'll get used to it.'

'You promise?' he said hopefully, and she nodded.

'The olive grove's over here,' she said, turning onto a track springy with tree debris. 'What's left of it.' She stopped to flip over a beetle floundering on its back. It was one of those summer beetles, all lit up with iridescent blue and green. Pretty, but just a beetle, Nick thought. She picked it up, letting it crawl along her arm. 'It's so pretty, and it's just a beetle.' She went over to put it on a tree trunk. 'Now some bird can come and pick it off.'

'My kind of girl,' he said with a shudder.

It was cool beneath the silver leaves of the olive trees. The fruit was hard, green and pendulous. Nick thought the black fingers she'd spoken of so lovingly in the pub only made the trees appear shrivelled and tortured, though it could have been due to the dimming light. 'I don't think an olive tree is one of the best things in the world,' he said, reaching for her. 'I think you are.'

'You know it's too late for you to head home tonight,' she said.

'Will your father mind?'

'He probably won't notice,' she said, leading him back the way they'd come.

Nick hoped he wouldn't notice that his daughter had been making love with a stranger down by the river, either. The memory sent a shudder through him and he was about to reach for her again when she flitted ahead to kick a stick out of his way. He let his hand drop. They might have just made love, but he wasn't yet familiar enough with her to reach out any old time.

'I guess you never get used to it, all this, the river, the trees,' he said, taking his cue from Robbie.

'I'm used to it.' She turned to face him, walking backwards lightly. 'You think this is where my rockabilly roots are?'

'Rockabilly, country, I don't know where roots come from,' he said. 'I'm from the city.'

'Apart from my mother, I wouldn't know, either. I only associated with olive pickers.'

'Was Max an olive picker?'

'His father was. I grew up with Max, in a seasonal sort of way, a bit like Robbie.' She took hold of a handlebar and pushed the bike with him. 'Only Max still lives here, works for the stock agent. His father taught me to drive.'

'Why didn't your father?'

'Bruno?' For a moment she seemed puzzled. 'I suppose he wasn't around.'

They stopped at the edge of a clearing. She made no move to go on, so they stood a while, sharing the last orange and staring across to the silhouette of trees outlined by a rising moon. Nick tried to see beyond the trees, but the shadows behind them were impenetrable, so he focused on the clearing. It was about ten metres across, he reckoned. There was no flake of bark, or leaf, or pellet of dung lying there, and he thought that whatever strayed into the circle must get swept away, that the purpose of the clearing was not so much to hold back the bush as a lesson in housekeeping. In the centre was a darker patch, the remains of an old campfire. The place was grim, and he wanted to crack a joke, that he and Robbie could learn a thing or two about cleaning the shed, but when he turned to Jude her profile was so melancholy that he reached over and touched her tangled hair instead.

'This is where my mother would sing. The pickers would sit around and teach her their songs. What I remember most about them is that they all had ripped fingernails and lumpy veins in their hands. I used to think they could break rocks with their fingers.'

A memorial, then. She was going somewhere he couldn't. 'Who keeps it so clear?' he asked, letting his hand fall from her hair. *Come back to me*, he wanted to say, *we're just beginning.*

'Bruno,' she said. 'It's about all he does these days.'

She made her way across the clearing, around the old fireplace, and through the trees. Now he could see that it was only a rebellious outcrop of rivergums, and on the other side was an old white Kingswood station wagon. It was parked beside the remains of a vegetable garden, staked out with faded twine hung with strips of rags. She noticed him looking at the Kingswood, and said, 'I don't drive it.' She took his hand and led him towards a small house of greying weatherboard.

'Welcome to the family home.'

A soft orangey light spread through the wire screen door from the hallway and over a verandah that sloped towards the ground. The house could have been mistaken for a temporary home if it hadn't been so worn out. Something moved in the corner of Nick's vision, the walls of what he'd taken to be a chicken shed.

'The mosquito house,' she told him.

'You breed mosquitoes?' He peered at the loose mesh walls that undulated as if someone inside had brushed an arm against them, but it was only a breeze coming up.

'We'll sleep there to get away from them,' she said, forgiving his flat joke with a flatter giggle.

The screen door clanged as somebody with a lantern came out of the house. The person approaching them didn't look like a Bruno. Brunos were brawny and brown and aggressively jolly. This man resembled a Peter Pan, a grown-up with a body in permanent protest about it, his legs jerking ahead of the rest of him. He was thin and brittle, and though his eyes and hair were as dark as Jude's, his skin wasn't. Nor was it reddish and windblown like every other farmer in the area. It was the colour of the chalky moths dive-bombing his lantern. He raised his hand in greeting to Nick, but hesitated when he saw Jude, as if he'd forgotten she lived there. Bruno brought with him a strangely pleasant smell of dust and chickenfeed, a homely smell. He raised the lantern to more clearly see Nick's face.

'You found your way,' he said. 'Not so easy if you don't do it every day.' His voice was soft, though too low-pitched for a Peter Pan, and his heavy accent gave a fluttery rhythm to his speech, as if he were giving a blessing.

'I got as far as the turn-off. Jude steered me the rest of the way.' He slapped at mosquitoes and waited for Jude to introduce them. She didn't say anything. Yet Bruno seemed content to hold the lantern high and grin at Nick, as if it were normal that Jude should ignore him.

'Tell him who I am,' he said, nudging Jude.

She started. 'This is Nick. He'll be staying in the mozzie house.'

'Yes,' Bruno said, keeping his eyes on Jude. 'Judit, it's long past time you had a visit.' He was gazing at her with a kind of awe, or maybe it was only the shadows thrown across his face by the lantern.

'The dogs aren't back yet,' she said.

'They'll come,' Bruno said, looking at Nick. 'Nothing for them out there.' He reeled towards the house and they straggled behind in the wake of the lantern.

'He doesn't look like anybody's father,' Nick whispered to her. 'What's his accent?'

'Hungarian. Can't you tell from looking at us?'

'No, should I?'

'No.' She stopped to laugh, pulling him to her so that his body enveloped her. Up this close, she was smaller than she seemed. He buried his face in her hair again; it didn't smell of shampoo, it didn't even smell clean. It smelled of earth and leaves and sweat and he almost gasped at how it made his blood rush.

The verandah groaned as they crossed it and entered a narrow hallway. There was a room off each side of the hall. Bruno hung the lantern in the doorway of one, and Nick stole a look into it. An open, empty, wardrobe, and a male smell emanating from rumpled sheets on a double bed. The door of the other room, presumably Jude's, was closed and he was glad now, seeing how close it was to Bruno's, that they would be sleeping outside. Nick followed Jude into the kitchen at the end of the hall. A pot was bubbling on the wood stove; stewing fish by the smell of it.

The kitchen was dominated by an enormous table. Jude led him to the end furthest from the heat of the stove. The air was just bearably hot, and a few bugs and moths had weaselled their way through the window screens. They fluttered around the soft light of a kerosene lamp that Bruno pumped to brighten the room before taking off his boots and putting them beside a wheezing gas-powered fridge. The wall behind Nick was lined with shelves that bowed under the weight of books with foreign titles. In front of the books was a row of figurines, carved from marble, limestone and granite, all of them fat-bellied women with breasts the shape of olives. Another wall was pegged with nails from which hung a number of checked flannel shirts, overalls, a hat and a coat. It looked as if Bruno had packed up and moved into the kitchen.

There was nothing of Jude here. Nick had expected a home, he supposed, with a bit of family tension and affection and bad jokes, normal stuff like his own. The air was pungent with fish soup, but beneath it he could smell the wariness separating these two. Whatever its cause, he guessed it kept the pin in the grenade.

There was grit on the floor. A small heap of stones lay on the table. The rough shape of a woman was emerging from a lump of granite, olive-breasted and similar to the figures on the bookshelf. He picked up the woman, surprised by the weight and the way it nuzzled itself into the curve of his palm. When he looked up, Bruno was frowning at something, not him, but Nick put the figure down. Beside the stones was a book about seashores and shells, the kind of watery book you needed out here in the dry country. He turned to the title page and read the name sprawled in childish letters across the page in red ink: *Judit Brack age eight.*

Jude flicked on the light switch, killing the Gothic atmosphere. She cleared one end of the table while Bruno ladled out bowls of the steaming fishy liquid from the pot; then she moved Nick to the cleared end and sat beside him. Under the table her leg sought his and hooked it, which set his pulse racing.

'From our river,' Bruno said, setting the bowls before them. 'Catfish soup.'

'Thanks, Mr Brack.' He was starving, but all he wanted to do was go with Jude to the mosquito house.

'I am Bruno.' He said it like a line of verse, though it sounded more absent-minded than deliberate. 'Eat up, eat up.'

'It's good,' Jude reassured him, so he ate up.

There came a frantic scratching and yowling from the verandah. Jude jumped up, nearly taking Nick's leg with her.

'The dogs.'

The hallway swallowed her and Nick was left staring at his soup, which tasted so good he didn't want it to end, but nor did he want to be left alone with Bruno, who'd picked up the stone woman-in-progress. The figurines reminded Nick of Cliff's line of antique phones in the shed. What was it about fathers, always in progress on a work?

'What kind of stone do you use for carving?' Nick asked at last.

'Local stone.'

Nick examined his thumbnails. *Come back and save me, Jude.* The night was still yelling outside, but here at the table silence hung between him and Bruno like a soggy sheet.

'So you've come to help Judit give her apologies to my wife?'

'Pardon?'

'She has no grave,' Bruno said, stroking the head of the figurine. 'She had ashes, but they're gone. Judit threw them away.'

More than the confusion of his words, Nick was startled by the bitterness that would make him say that about his daughter. But all he saw in Bruno's face was sadness, and that made him even more uneasy. He wondered what he'd walked into; he wondered if Robbie could have warned him.

He stood up. 'Where's the toilet, please?'

'Out back,' Bruno said. He opened the door off the kitchen and ushered Nick through into the night.

There was an outhouse, and probably a light, but Nick wasn't ready to sally forth. He could hear Jude's voice coming from the direction of the mosquito house, chiding the dogs. While he took his leak by a tree, he gaped up at the sky and his scalp prickled. With no town lights out here to dim them, there were more stars than he'd ever seen. He peered into the darkness and caught sight of the river. There was the moon, glowering at him from the ripples on the surface. Then Jude was beside him, sending ripples across his own surface, as she led him to the mosquito house.

The dogs stood guard. Nick offered his hand to them to sniff, but they turned their heads.

'They'll get used to you,' Jude said.

He hoped so. If the dogs hated him, he was lost.

It was a simple sleeping place; a framed net around a large sleeping mat. Damp hessian bags that smelled a little swampy hung from the back wall, cooling the air. Now that his eyes had adjusted to the dark he reached out to touch the mesh wall, poking at it, testing for holes. 'Tell me you weren't lying about snakes sleeping at night.' He took another breath and added, 'Your father said you ditched your mother's ashes.'

'Don't worry about snakes, and I didn't throw out Leni's ashes. I buried them under a tree.'

'Why didn't you tell him?'

'I did. He thinks it's the same as chucking them. He wants them on the bookshelf.' She pulled him down to the mat. She lay on her side to face him, playing with his fingers. 'Listen, I want to tell you this story.'

10

IT WAS ANOTHER OPPRESSIVELY BLUE AND GOLD SUMMER DAY. Bert Jawframe had been discharged after breakfast. Phil had unscrewed the steel halo from Bert's cheekbones, leaving a little hole in each cheek. At last Bert's jaw was free, and his lips parted, but only to take a breath.

'They'll scar, those holes, but just a bit,' Phil told him. 'A little something to remind you of the occupational hazards of roofing.'

'Bye-bye, Bertie,' Eric sang. 'Time to change your trade.'

'Good luck and all that,' Nick chorused.

Hunched over a walking frame to take the weight off his pelvis, Bert had simply delivered a sidelong glare, then scraped his way across the room and through the door in pained silence.

Al was still sleeping off last night's injection. Eric heaved a sigh and turned back to his magazine, pretending that Al's distress hadn't affected him. It was a long-term 24-hour-a-day relationship with Eric, and understanding his signals the way he did, Nick realised he'd never learnt a thing about Jude's.

He stared out the window, wondering what kind of life was going on outside. Five minutes later he was still deciding whether the hospital was situated in a street or a paddock; all he could remember of the town were a couple of twittering girls and an Emporium. He needed something to help distract him from the life he was caught in. Listening to Roy would only make it worse, but there was the talking book Robbie brought him – he could let somebody else's life and problems entertain him. It was in the drawer, with the other CDs, waiting for somebody to come and hook him up, waiting for him to remember to ask them to do it. When Phil came in on the drug round Nick asked him to plug him in.

'Are you sure that's a story?' he asked, squinting at the title Phil held up: *The Shipping News*.

'It'll suck you in,' Phil said, putting the earphones in his ears, 'or it'll send you to sleep.' He pressed the play button and cast his eyes around the room. 'Either way, you win.'

Nick took a deep breath, closed his eyes and settled in for it as a woman displaced the other voice that lived in his head to tell him about a bumbling man called Coil who had feet as big as Nick's by the sounds of it. He saw himself, suddenly, simply walking; at the same time his legs remembered what it was like and twitched with yearning. The longing to walk, to stand, to bend, nearly made him howl. But there was nothing to be done about it, and he subsided back into the story. These days, he could appreciate the way the narrator used her voice, rhythmic and soothing, not putting him to sleep, only preparing him for the next word. The thought infused him with melancholy; it came from Jude, this recognition of vocal subtleties. Again, there was nothing to be done, and eventually his gloom made room for anticipation as the narrator's words unfurled the story.

As Coil was about to lose his job, a man arrived at Al's bed and pulled the curtain around. The earphones blocked off anything Nick might have heard, and Eric was sleeping, so he went back to the story. Coil was heading for rock bottom when the man leaned over Nick's face and gently pulled the earphones from his ears. He placed them on the bedside table, but didn't turn the player off. The narrator continued Coil's adventures without Nick.

'Hello Nick, I'm Len Buckle.'

The stand-in for Al's shrink. He was wearing a bad tie and too much aftershave. 'I didn't send for you,' Nick said.

Len Buckle chuckled. 'Hardly anybody does.' He drew the curtain, pulled up the chair and sat without asking, without any hesitation, as if he'd never needed permission to intrude on a stranger's life. 'I'm following up the episode with Mr Alpen – you're not being accused of anything,' he said quickly, when Nick looked confused.

'Oh, you mean Al.'

'I just wanted to reassure you that, while we appreciate your concern for Mr Alpen, all care is given to our patients.'

Nick took his time examining the slashes and squiggles on Len's tie while he wondered where the guy was heading. 'Okay,' he said.

'I'm also following up staff reports. My presence is standard procedure and, of course, you're here because of certain circumstances . . . withdrawal, aggression, these can simply occur due to sleep disturbance.'

'Withdrawal? I can't withdraw,' Nick said gaping pointedly at his plaster. Not like Al who could wind himself into a ball of nothingness. 'I don't think I can be aggressive, either.'

'And we wondered whether you could give the date of your parents' return to the country?' Len said, not missing a beat. 'You'd be better off, in all ways, rehabilitating at home.'

Len Buckle's tie was an X-ray of his brain, Nick decided. He felt himself diminishing, sinking into juvenility without Jude to keep him grown up. 'I don't have the exact date, but it's in about two weeks – and I should be out by then, anyway.' The curtains were drawn, but he could feel Eric listening in, picturing Len's sceptical scrutiny of Nick's pulley contraption. Do the maths, he told himself, but he couldn't remember exactly how long he'd been in – it was all one long day, one endless night. Lindy would know. Two weeks to recover was cutting it fine, but he'd make it, he'd have to. Just as Len opened his mouth to speak Eric started his routine.

'Nurse, nurse!' he yelled. 'Where's my bottle, where's my bedpan?' Jumping in on cue with his loud distractions, protecting Nick from the bogeyman, saving him from the hard bits.

'I'm really tired, Len,' Nick said. 'After last night's episode and all.'

'Well, I'm glad we had this talk, Nick. I'm glad to get to know you better.' Len opened the curtains to reveal Eric slapping his own cheeks in frustration.

'Bloody flies!' he howled.

'A bit of nature,' Len said mildly. 'We don't often see it in here.'

'Nature? Bloody flies around your sick bed, can't wait till you're dead. Don't tell me about nature. I've got whopping great tomato plants pushing their way through my footpath – that's nature! You've got to beat it back with a stick.' Eric's tirade dwindled to a wheeze. 'It'll get you in the end, and when it does the flies are first in line.'

'At least you can still flick them off.' Nick only meant to sound affable, but Len Buckle shot him a look as if he were accusing him of being depressed – or worse, withdrawn. Maybe he was both of them, all this lurching from self-pity to anger and back to nothing at all except a fossilising body.

'I'll get the staff to look into the matter of your parents' return – I assume you've let them know of your situation?'

'Well, no,' Nick said. 'I didn't want to ruin their holiday and it's not like I'm dying.'

'But somebody else might be,' Len said, 'and you'd be taking up their bed.'

Nick's eyes slid towards Bert's empty bed, but didn't say anything. Even he knew accidents happened just like that.

'Shrinks,' Eric spluttered as Len's footsteps made their jaunty way down the hall. 'Poking their noses into places they've got no business being. You're better off with a few beers and a fag.'

'They haven't helped you much,' Nick scowled at him, the goodwill from the night before gone. 'It's your bloody fault – I reckon that nurse set him onto me for *your* threat to shoot Al.'

'No!' Eric seemed surprised rather than sorry. 'It was sending for Lindy that did it.'

'That wasn't aggressive!'

'Well none of it was withdrawal.' Eric shrugged. 'Beats me. Of course I'm sorry, but I don't think you need to worry. As soon as your family's back, you get to go home.'

Nick grunted. 'I should've kept my gob shut, and you should've, too.'

'Don't be so hard,' Eric said. 'Sometimes I don't hear my own drivel because I'm off somewhere else – not with the pixies,' he added quickly, 'just another place. You never think it'll come to this when you're young. You wake up one morning and you're forty. You wake up the next morning, you're eighty, and all your mistakes and bad habits have made the trip with you.'

There was so much regret, a lifetime's worth, in his weary old eyes that Nick had to shut it out. 'Eric, I reckon you're the bad habit.'

'Good or bad,' Eric said gloomily, 'we're each other's habit now. A sorry pair, waking up to each other every day. Where's that nurse?' He pressed the call button and Phil appeared almost instantly.

'Phil, you're a godsend. Can you help me out?' Eric pleaded. 'It's got to be the bathroom this time, I can't cop the sight of another bedpan.'

'See all this metal around you?' Phil said. 'It means you're attached to the bed. You're in traction, Eric, just like Nick. You don't go anywhere. Everything comes to you, including the bog.' He hooted his big laugh. 'Like a king.'

'Bloody monarchist. Get me a bedpan, then – and warm it up, or I'll be getting piles again.'

Listening with half an ear, Nick tried to put aside the potential problems posed by Len Buckle. Once again, the implications of what he'd done were occurring to him too late, and once again, he decided to deal with it later. A tinny buzz in the air brought the needed distraction; it wasn't a fly, but the narrator, stuck in his earphones with the story. When Phil came back with Eric's bedpan, Nick asked him for help.

'Better than listening to the old fart, eh?' Phil murmured before plugging the earphones in.

He didn't answer immediately. Although Eric wouldn't have heard, these things had become important – you had to weigh the risk of rough handling against loyalty. The problem was that they were all clinchers. The clincher was the thought of Nurse Sunni's stinging, flicking sheets; the clincher was that he had to look at Eric – and Iris – more often than have his bed changed; the clincher was that he didn't want the hospital to throw him onto the street. As a gesture of apology he gave Eric and Phil big smiles before putting the dilemma away with all his others. 'Can you wind it back a way, Phil, it's been going all the time.'

Phil pressed it cheerfully. 'The rewind button is one of my favourite things.'

'I know what you mean.' Nick had gone through the whole dilemma thing and Phil had already forgotten about it. Nothing lasted here.

The narrator towed him back into the story. He listened and imagined, and in the pauses between the chapters he waited, and gradually slid into sleep. When he woke one of the earphones had fallen from his ear and lucky Coil was living in another place.

11

'ONCE THERE WAS A WOMAN WHO WANTED TO THREAD A needle, but her fingers had a mind of their own. She held the needle out to the daughter and asked, "Why can't I thread it?" The daughter told her it was the needle's fault, that the eye was too small for threading. But the woman struggled with the needle because she wanted to mend her husband's overalls. But then she got so angry she cast the needle to the floor. The daughter snatched it up before the mother could bring her foot down on her hand. The daughter threaded the needle, pretending it was hard, though it was a needle for sewing leather, with an eye as big as a grain of rice. She gave the threaded needle to her mother, who stared at it and said, "What do I do with this, Dearness?"'

Between sentences, phrases, and sometimes between two words, Jude paused. She had no fear of silence. Nick listened to the story, but it was her pauses that kept him attentive, the ease of them, like taking in air. Unlike his own, they were never an attempt, usually futile, to find the next words. He wondered if he could ever acquire that sense of timing himself, or if it was in the blood.

'It's about me of course, and Leni,' Jude went on. 'I'd answer to Dearness as if it was my real name, not some word from an old song. Then she forgot that I was Dearness.'

Waiting for a silence to pass, he wondered again about her easy pauses. She was a singer, she knew how to breathe, but where was her pain? He took her hand. It was cold and slippery with sweat. There it was. Then she was drawing him to her, curling over, around and beneath him, his skin under her nails, urgent, but still holding something back. He had time; he could wait for all of her.

𝄞

The next day Nick asked her to sing for him. She did immediately, a ballad he'd never heard before. He loved the way she didn't have to be talked into it. 'Leni sang, and so do I,' she told him. 'It's what I do – even if I am still searching for my own voice.' Then she broke into a rocky old Beatles number, 'Can't Buy Me Love'. It was one that Cliff used to sing, and Nick joined her, Jude's voice leaning into his, propping it up.

'I used to think of the things you inherit,' she said when the song ended. 'Like your feet or a bad temper, and I thought my voice was one of those things, that I couldn't do anything to change it. Leni taught me to sing, but I think a voice is something you can develop yourself.'

'Some of us need a little help from our friends,' he quipped.

Her eyes gleamed as she tapped him on the chest. 'You should have a go singing at the pub – everybody does it.'

'You mean I get to act out my teenage fantasy?'

'I'll give you some singing lessons,' she said, adding with a giggle, 'You can't be worse than Frank and Sue.'

Nick nodded, thinking nobody could murder a song like they did. But they did it with feeling.

When Bruno came in they all toyed with the mess that Nick had cooked up. He'd offered in a moment of misplaced optimism, thinking he'd remember something of what Maree had tried to teach him. He didn't. Later, they left Bruno carving stones at the table. Jude took Nick into her room for a lesson. He could see why she slept in the mosquito house. The bed was stacked with vinyl records, CDs and a couple of bruised guitars. There was one of those swivelling office chairs, which she'd draped with green velvet, and there was a shelf stacked with more CDs and songbooks. Jude's clothes, the cowgirl outfit and some flimsy dresses, hung from a picture rail on the wall. Beneath them was an ancient drum machine that looked more mechanical than electronic. Another guitar with bits falling off it rested against a speaker. He'd need a map of all the power-boards and cables and extension cords just to get to the bed. She could have had all that stuff on a computer, but there was no high-tech here.

'There's only one power point,' she said, following his gaze. 'And I like the tone of this old equipment.' On the floor was a record player even older than the one Maree had tossed from the shed years ago. It was the kind that looked as if it had to be wound to get it going, and he gave a low whistle of appreciation. And there, like a sign, heading up the stack of records against the wall, was Roy Orbison.

'You don't have exclusive rights to him,' she said.

Nick wanted to ask about the records, but Jude motioned for him to sit in the swivelling chair. Everything appeared as flimsy as her clothes; all set to fall apart, including the walls, but it also seemed precious. On the wall above the records was a photograph of a woman with burning eyes as green as a palm tree. She had only just stopped being young, and her expression was startled, as if she'd suddenly realised an awful mistake. She looked like a grown-up kid about to topple off a wardrobe, and she must be Leni.

'Your mother's pretty,' he said.

'Yes. Those are her records. They're all I've got left of her, records and instructions on how to sing and how to behave.' Her focus shifted to the window and stayed a moment, perhaps caught by her own reflection. 'Sometimes it feels like there's a ghost inside me.'

'You don't look like you're haunted.' Nick reached out to touch her mass of hair. 'Your hair's too dark.'

Suddenly she was standing in front of him, putting her hands on his shoulders and hauling him from the chair by the sleeves of his T-shirt, as if he were something for the laundry basket.

'How's your breathing?'

'My what?'

'Your breathing.' She pushed his shoulders back with her fingertips. 'You have to know how to breathe before you can sing. It's the same as learning to think before you speak.'

'I think all right. It just doesn't help. Anyway, I thought singers never did that. I thought we were supposed to open our mouths and let it all out.'

'You've got to know *what* to let out and how to express it – how to emote.' She was being thorny, prodding his shoulders. 'But first you've got to breathe. Straighten your back.'

It was like preparing for a marathon. Big yawns, sighs and neck bends, getting the breath ready for its trip. 'You do all this?' he gasped between vowels, irked by the dribbles they produced. She stopped, surprised.

'Well, yes, but I've never thought much about it until now – you're my first pupil.'

He dribbled and sprayed some more; trying to breathe her way felt unnatural, but Jude kept him at it, casually wiping his spittle from her cheek. She switched him to lip flutters that turned his dribbles into a waterspout. She made him bend from the waist and do little siren *eeee*s as he rose that set the dogs howling and his teeth on edge.

'Where'd you get those dogs?' he asked, just to get a breather.

'Somebody dumped them.'

It was hard work, but eventually his vocal cords were relaxed, his head was crackling with nervous energy, and he hadn't sung a note.

'What do you want to sing?'

'A Roy Orbison song.'

'Maybe go for something simpler on your first night,' Jude told him after he sang her the first few bars of 'Working for the Man'. What they finally settled on was 'Blue Moon', something Roy had never done. A crooning song, smooth and melancholy, older than retro, more antique than Jude's drum machine, it was one of those songs he'd always known – it would have been among the lullabies Maree had sung to him, and she'd have delivered it to Bowie, too – Maree didn't have a big repertoire. Jude picked up one of the guitars and played with him. When he finished the song he was pleased that his voice didn't crack as much as it usually did, but Jude didn't look overjoyed.

'You can hold a tune.' The faint doubt in her voice battered him with every syllable. 'You'd be all right at harmonies, but your tone's patchy and your voice isn't very strong.'

'It's stronger than yours.'

'No, you're just shouting to make it louder.'

He believed her.

'If you've got a voice, you'll find it.' She said it bluntly, as if his voice might be hiding under a stone. 'But we're doing this for fun – you're only singing at The Fat Stag.' Jude was teaching him, doing for him what she'd said her mother did for her, and then it was up to him. She seemed to be looking vacantly at him, but then said, 'I'm learning too, you know.'

12

WHEN IRIS ARRIVED AT FOUR O'CLOCK, ERIC'S BED WAS empty. Her patient eyes flickered with fright, but then a streak of relief crossed her face. When she looked at Nick she seemed more interested in his swollen red eye than in what might have happened to Eric.

'I've got a sty and Eric's gone for an X-ray,' he told her. 'He said to tell you if he's not back in half an hour to call Franz Kafka.' He looked at her uncertainly. 'He said you'd know what he meant.'

Iris nodded.

Lingering by Eric's bed to slyly straighten the bottom sheet, she nodded again to herself before shuffling over in her jiffy slippers to sit with Nick. She took *Who* from her bag and laid it on his bed, turning it so both of them could see. Slowly, slowly, she turned the pages, while Nick scanned the pictures and captions.

'What did he mean by Kafka?'

'Oh, he's got the holy terrors about disappearing under red tape – Kafka wrote a bit about the subject.'

'You've actually read him?'

'Goodness yes, love. You don't get to marry Eric without reading Kafka.'

Not even Robbie had been able to force Nick into reading that guy. He gaped at her. Nobody was what they seemed. Iris turned another page and together they took in the pictures silently, amiably. When they came to a schlock-horror article about Kurt Cobain, Iris said, 'That boy always looked tortured.'

'He was an all-right singer, though.' Nick never liked him much, but you had to defend the brotherhood. 'I sang a bit, too. Once.'

'I can see why you changed your mind,' Iris said, peering at Kurt's face, which was ravaged more likely by the cruel camera than by his life.

'I didn't change my mind.'

She looked at him expectantly.

'Well, I sang once. In Crundle.'

'Oh, Crundle!' Iris exclaimed. 'I know Crundle, we lived there a while when our boy was little. Did you sing at the hotel? It was a church in our day, and there was such a to-do about its deconsecration and being turned into a pub . . .' She trailed off, staring at the wall as if that part of her life were being played out on it. 'But there was no parish left to speak of, and then we heard they started the talent nights. People settled down soon enough.'

'Did you know Bruno Brack? He had an olive farm.'

'Oh, we don't know anybody there now, this was nearly fifty years ago and the place would have turned over its population a dozen times since then. We lived in the village, while Eric was waiting for his position here.'

'What did he do?'

'He edited the *Left Bank*,' she said. 'Can you imagine? A socialist paper out here in those days.'

'Never heard of it,' Nick said, impressed nevertheless. Volcano-breath Eric, a rad commie editor.

'Well, it closed down years before your time. It went bankrupt, but all the best publications do, apparently,' she added wryly. 'But you were talking about singing, love. Is that what you want to be, a singer?'

'You mean what's my *knack*? I don't know. I'll think about it when I get out of here.'

'It sounds like you have a knack for avoiding knacks. But it won't be long now, love. I hear your parents will be home soon,' she said, turning another page. 'It must be lovely to take a holiday overseas. Did they go to Europe?'

Iris sat there, solid in her knitted tan cardigan, as rheumy as Eric, but with a sunnier nature, which must have come from reading all those magazines. It couldn't have come from reading Kafka. Her eyes were always an integral part of her smiles, like the one she gave him now. Her smiles were true.

'They didn't go anywhere.'

When Iris didn't bat an eyelid, it crossed his mind that Lindy had already told her, but he dismissed it immediately. Strange, how he knew she wouldn't have. 'They're at home. They think I'm still picking tomatoes.' Iris's face, etched with experience, was enough to make him believe that nothing would shock or disgust her. 'I couldn't tell them then, and I can't tell them now. It's too late. It'd kill them to know I didn't tell them, so I can't *ever* tell them. And how am I going to pull that off? Coming home after months of muscle-building fruit-picking with wasted arms and a gammy leg. I'll have to build myself up before I go back.' He blew out his cheeks in frustration. 'And now they want to chuck me out of here, and I'll still be in plaster. I'll just have to hole up somewhere. Or I could tell them I fell off a ladder – that happens with fruit-picking.'

Iris looked entirely unconvinced.

'Okay, you're right,' he said. 'But I don't have to tell them *when* it happened. But the other thing – using a bed that somebody else might need. I don't want to be the cause of someone's death.'

'Oh, don't worry about that,' Iris said. 'They'll just park you in the corridor on a trolley, same as they always do. They've done it to Eric often enough.'

'I think they just want to get rid of me.'

'Of course they do, love. That's their job. You shouldn't take it personally.' She closed the magazine. 'But no, they won't put you out on the street. The important thing is your family, and all the trouble of keeping a lie going. They'll expect stories of your adventures, and you won't have any. You'll have to make them up and you'll get them wrong because they won't be true.'

He thought of the stories Robbie might concoct for him in his emails. They'd want re-enactments. 'I'm pretty good at making stuff up.'

'And the pity of it is,' she went on, 'it's not as if you didn't have any stories from your bed.' She threw up her hands. 'It's a perilous voyage in here, sometimes.'

He closed his eyes as much as the sty would let him. He'd have to keep the whole sorry story a secret until one of those days thirty years down the track, when he'd say with a laugh, 'You remember that time I went fruit-picking and didn't come back for yonks?' The thought of thirty years made him smile grimly. Only a few weeks ago the idea of simply reaching the age of thirty was inconceivable. *Who'd want to live past thirty?* he'd said to Jude. *Take the test*, he'd said, as if it were a simple school exam. Now he could see thirty over there, glowing faintly like false dawns on both their horizons. His imagination wouldn't stretch to fifty. Not even with Iris before him, a living example of the other side of the horizon.

He opened his eyes to see if a solution had lit up her face.

'You might have to come clean, love.'

Nick considered the idea while Iris opened the magazine and found her place.

'There's this little question about shame and pride,' he told her. He thought he'd lost those two, ever since he stopped worrying about Nurse Sunni wiping his arse, but here they were looking like they'd just returned from a turn round the block. 'But I'll think about it.'

With an understanding smile, Iris turned the next page to a story about a suburban house fire. While Iris read the article, Nick studied the picture of a couple wrapped in blankets and standing among the ashes of their house. 'Smoking in bed's what started it,' she said. 'Eric's a smoker. It's killing him, but he won't have a bar of quitting.'

'My mother smokes when she's stressed out.' Another reason not to tell Maree anything.

'It's an awful habit, love. I was nearly driven to taking it up myself when I had our Joe. He was such a hard baby.'

'Eric's never mentioned kids,' he said, wondering if Trace would approve of his indirect line of approach. *You'll have to ask Eric*, she'd said. But Iris was Eric.

'We only had the one,' she said. 'He's gone.' From her bag she pulled out the plastic folder Eric was always sneaking a look at, and took a small photograph from it. Now Nick was in on his secret and he wasn't sure he wanted to be. But Iris gently placed the photograph on his lap. Ragged at the edges from handling, it showed a boy about four years old leaning against the slim legs of a woman he assumed was Iris when she was young, and he automatically examined her first. Her hair was done up in a big puff and her wide smile was so easy it seemed permanent. He looked at her now, searching for traces of her young face under the wrinkles and overgrown freckles; the smile was still wide, but there was no easiness. He turned back to the photograph of the child Joe, and he couldn't help trying to find something – in his frown, in his stance – in common with Bowie, the only person he could remember at four. The picture was too small, too finger-printed to see details like freckles, but Nick recognised the four-year-old ownership of his mother's legs.

'What's he holding?'

Iris leaned over and picked up the photograph, studying it as if for the first time. 'His catapult. Eric made two of them, one for Joe and one for himself. It was their favourite game for some time, shooting at each other with paper pellets.'

'That's why he told Al he'd shoot him.'

Her smile was small and puzzled, but she let it go. 'You never get over it, the loss of your child,' she murmured, slipping the photograph back into the folder. 'Somebody said to me once, "Imagine your son has gone to Paris, and sooner or later you will join him." I cried at that, but sometimes it helps a little bit.'

'How did he die?'

'He didn't. Oh no, he didn't die. He was conscripted into the army and sent to Vietnam in 1970. And he did come back.'

Her voice was drifting off. Nick could hear it being pulled down the achingly fresh trail of her memory. 'But he wasn't our Joe when he returned. He came back angry at everything and frightened of odd things, especially cats, I don't know why. We had to give our tabby away, and Joe used to love him. He'd walk all the streets around Marston, looking for things to be mad at or afraid of. People, mostly, and in the end a lot of them were frightened of him. He made a lot of people angry, too.' She stopped for breath. 'But you don't want to hear all this, love,' she said, continuing before Nick could say that he did. 'It went on for years and he came in here quite a few times, but they couldn't help him. Then one day he left and we never heard from him and nobody could find him. That was fifteen years ago. He'll be fifty-seven next month, and he's alive somewhere, we know it. We just wait for him.'

Nick followed her gaze out the window to the dull sky. Something about the window made the weather always look bad. Sneaking a peep at Iris's face, older than he'd imagined, he was struck with wonder and respect that she could bear her loss. It was worse, somehow, than if Joe were dead. He wanted to ask her, what's worse, knowing or not-knowing, but was afraid of her reaction, that she'd cry, and he wouldn't be able to stroke her hand. He was afraid of saying how sorry he was for her.

'Do you have pictures of him as an adult?' he asked.

'A lot of pictures, but this is the one Eric likes best,' she said, patting her bag. 'You know, love, Eric never gets to talk to young people these days, the most he can hope for is that somebody like you gets put next to him in hospital, somebody who'll answer back, but can't walk away. And he likes the girls visiting Al. They knew Joe – Lindy was only a girl then, but she remembers him, and Tracie's a few years older so she knew him quite well.'

'So they really have been coming here all their lives?'

'A good bit of it – off and on.' She noticed his red eye again, and grimaced with sympathy.

'The nurse is bringing me some ointment.'

'Gold is the thing for a sty.' Tugging at her wedding ring, she managed to slide it over her swollen knuckle. 'I'm going to run this along your eyelid, love, and it'll be fixed up in no time. Close your eye.'

He closed both of them while Iris rubbed the thin gold band against his eyelid. He couldn't feel any difference, but it wasn't making it any worse either, so he let her keep at it. Her breath, smelling faintly of tea, fanned his face as she talked.

'Eric always whipped himself over Joe being lost to us. Joe just going like that nearly killed him. Eric seemed to decide he wasn't suffering enough, and every job he did, he'd make it as hard as he could. Little things, something he could have built in the shed, he'd do at the bottom of the yard without a hat or shirt, just to scorch himself in the sun. Then he'd lug the pieces back to the shed and put it together there. He was bent on making life more of a misery for himself than it already was. He'd have walked with barbed wire in his shoes if I'd let him.' She paused, momentarily lifting the ring from his eyelid. 'The thing was, he saw me as a comfort, and that made him keep away. We only had each other, but sometimes it was like we'd lost different sons, we were so far apart.' She stopped rubbing, and Nick opened his eyes to see the wedding ring slide effortlessly back over her knuckle. 'It's always easier going on than coming off.'

Iris could say the most obvious thing, he thought, that somehow managed to hit him, like a stone hidden in a snowball. He could ponder that one for hours, he knew, and in the end decide that what she said was what she meant: a ring is easier to slip on than pull off.

'That eye will be better in the morning,' she said. 'You wait and see – some old wives' tales are true.'

'You never told a true tale in your life, you old wive,' Eric screeched as his trolley came through the door.

'See? We've survived, in a way.' She gathered up her bag to go to Eric. 'Tell your parents, love,' she whispered. 'They'll forgive everything, especially little things like shame and pride.'

Nick nodded, looking at Eric with new interest, and admiration – for the truth of his claim to have done something for society, to have done without Joe, same as Iris. Only he wasn't the same as Iris. He should have asked Eric about Joe, like Trace said. But then he'd have heard a different story.

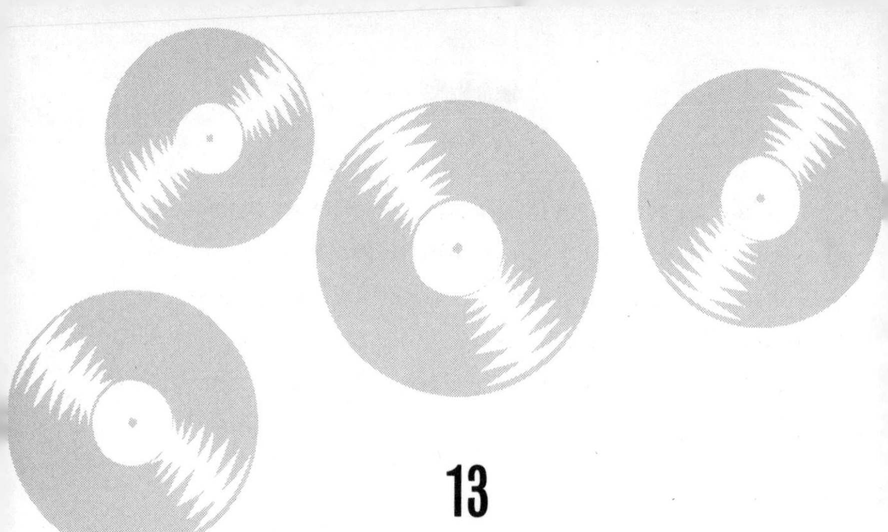

13

The punch landed on the side of Nick's face. His head floundered as he tried to focus on Robbie's face and on what had happened. It was Monday morning in the picking fields, and his smooth, imperturbable mate had come at him with his arm swinging.

Nick had set off for the tomato fields at dawn, supplied for the journey with oranges and long kisses from Jude. She'd led him out of the mosquito house and through the maze of trees that he didn't reach out to touch this time because there was Jude's skin to set his fingers aflutter, to breathe on, before she sent him on his way. Riding across the plain in the cool thin air, he'd listened to the soft tremolo gliding around the space where his brain used to be, telling him there was nothing he couldn't do, no problem that couldn't wait.

Heading into the watery red sunrise, he rode directly to the fields. Robbie and the others were picking already, boxes of tomatoes marking their progress down the rows. As he parked the bicycle under the tree where they sat for their breaks, Angie threw a handful of tomatoes into her box and came over for some water.

'Is that all you've picked in two days?' he said jokingly, indicating her half-full box.

'It's all I've managed in a week,' she said as sourly as her Irish lilt allowed. 'There must be an easier way to trek around the world.' She took another slug of water from her bottle. 'Enough sweat to baptise you,' she muttered, shaking her dripping face. With a lethargic wave she ambled back down her row. On the way she said something to Robbie, who was working the row alongside hers. Robbie straightened up and walked over to Nick, who could not keep the grin off his face.

'You're looking pretty smug for a yob,' he said. When Nick kept smiling to himself, Robbie's eyes narrowed. 'Have a good look around did you?'

'What's it to you? You've got yours.' He indicated with his chin towards Angie.

Robbie didn't flinch, his voice remained even. 'Jude's a mate.' He stood back, a sneer playing on his lips. Nick knew that stance; once again Robbie was calculating Nick's level of stupidity. Then he said softly, 'You're still pissed off about Emma.'

'Nope, I'm not . . .'

'Revenge,' Robbie went on, 'is not a good a reason to be with somebody. She'll bite you.'

The smile faded from Nick's face. 'You're so full of it, and you can't figure it out – you've got top spot on the pecking order and I've got Jude.'

'Yeah,' Robbie drawled. 'So what's she see in you?'

For a moment Nick wondered. *What did she see?* A good bloke, attentive, floundering a bit, but not too much trouble. Apart from the floundering it was pretty much what he'd thought he'd seen in her – only she was turning out to be not so simple. He could feel Robbie watching, waiting for a flash of doubt to pounce on, so he kept his eyes on the ground. It was Robbie who'd once told him that lust was relative. The hots come at different temperatures, he'd said, and burn at different levels, the heart, the cock, the mind. But this was deeper. Robbie had never mentioned the level below the hots.

'It's a bit more than lust.'

'Yeah, the caring guy. I heard you give her the Bowie story,' Robbie said. 'I heard you playing the clucking hen.'

Nick raised his head, squinting in the metallic sunlight. 'What's that supposed to mean?'

Robbie's laugh was scornful. 'Mate! You milk that Time Warp story every time.'

'It's not a story, it's the truth.'

'That kid's got more street smarts than you. You either don't know him or you're using him to get laid. And you don't know Jude – you'd better not be using her.'

'It's not about you, or revenge for Emma. You're talking shit. I like Jude – a lot. I know she's not fooled by your sleaze – she knows you. And I know enough. I know her mother's dead.'

'Maybe you should ask her for the rest of the story.'

'Why don't you just keep out of it? You haven't seen her since you were ten.'

'She was a mate then and she's a mate now.'

Nick took a step towards him. 'So am I.'

'So what's the problem?' Robbie asked. They'd reached the impasse, and now stood warily, eyeing each other.

'You're the one with the problem,' Nick said. 'Your two *mates* are on together and you're out of the loop.' That was when Robbie's arm came swinging.

𝄞

'That's awful,' Jude said, applying a compress to Nick's blackening eye.

'And that's not all of it,' he said. 'I trip over, fall onto the brick, and I'm so out of it when I go to bed that I chuck my clothes over the mosquito coil. Next thing, I wake up, that thunderstorm's cracking over my head, the place is full of smoke and both of us are gasping – the water's outside and we can't find the bucket.'

'What did you do?' Distracted by the story, Jude pressed the cloth harder against his eye.

'We slit the grain sacks,' Nick said, trying not to wince. 'We dragged them over and buried the fire and my clothes under half a ton of wheat.'

She laughed so hard that he nearly writhed under the pressure of her shaking hand. 'Tony'll make you pay for that grain.'

'Yeah. It was only a little fire, but everything had been smouldering for hours.'

Jude removed the compress and he relaxed in the chair, rolling Bruno's carved stone-woman in his palm. 'So I bailed and came here.' He cleared his throat. 'I thought it was better to let Robbie cool off after I nearly torched his uncle's shed.'

'All that lightning last night, it must've been a hairy ride,' she said, bringing them both coffee. 'How'd you find your way through the trees?'

'It was nearly daylight by then.' He put the stone-woman down and wrapped his hands around the coffee mug. 'So can I stay?' Alarm crossed her face so fast he decided he'd misread everything. 'Just a couple of days?' He waited while she thought about it, absently combing her hair with her fingers.

Robbie may or may not back up his story about falling onto the brick, though the fire was true. There had been an uneasy truce by the end of the day – after all, they had to share a shed – but no forgiveness on either side. Their sullenness had built up at the same rate as the storm clouds, and Nick supposed that it would continue until either Nick stopped seeing Jude, or Robbie got used to it, or stole her from him. He hoped that the only possibility was the middle option. Robbie should just have to wear it.

He'd set off for Jude's in dull anger. Robbie hadn't chucked him out, but Nick hadn't wanted to stay there. The storm was dry and rumbling; he'd pedalled beneath red and bronze sheets of lightning that revealed the scale of the sky, how moody it was, and how easily it could snuff him out. He'd imagined himself a creeping speck, something Lola Starke wouldn't bother to shoot at. He'd pedalled furiously, thinking how futile his anger was and how he couldn't let it go yet because it was fuelling the journey to Jude's. By the time he'd turned into the misty trees, he and the sky were calm, and the mosquito-coil fire had turned into one of those lucky strokes that got him back to her.

'All right,' she said at last. 'A couple of days – Bruno can cope with that. What about your job?'

'Can I pick olives?'

'They won't be ready for weeks – it's back to the tomatoes for you.'

'Riding two hours each way . . .'

'If Tony lets you keep the bike.'

'I could call him,' Nick said reaching into his pocket for his mobile. It wasn't there. 'It's in my other pants, buried under the wheat.'

She shook her head. 'Wouldn't work out here, anyway. And the landline's down from the storm. It'll be a few hours before they fix it.' She broke some eggs into an electric pan. 'I've got to go to work. Max is picking me up in half an hour . . . you can ride in with us. Bring the bike, in case Tony wants it back. Stay and pick, we'll get you on the way home.'

'You're so sensible,' he said admiringly. 'You could run my life for me.'

'Tell me you're not going to turn out to be another Bruno,' she said, flipping the eggs.

'Why do you stay here?' he asked.

'It's my home, too. I'll leave when I'm ready.' She put the plate of eggs on the table in front of him. 'Tomorrow, you cook.' They looked at each other doubtfully.

'My mother tried real hard to teach me,' Nick said. 'But I just wasn't interested.'

'Tomorrow you start being interested.'

Sometime in the night he was woken by the dogs whimpering outside. He rolled over to open the wire door for them, and after Jude kicked at them in her sleep they curled at his feet.

He was getting fond of them, in the way you become attached to a friend's weaknesses, though he was still chafing over the way they'd heeded Max this morning, responding to his voice and whistles with an obedience bordering on the devotion they gave Jude. With his porkpie tilted at a jaunty angle, Max was more flaky than cool, but he was Jude's old friend, more than Robbie ever was, and that counted for something. He'd taken Nick in and out of Tony's without once mentioning Nick's black eye, and that counted for something, too, even though he'd only done it for Jude.

Things were turning rosy. Tony had let him keep the bike while he worked for him, and would dock him a small sum for the two sacks of wheat. 'Just make sure you clean it up, the mess,' he'd told Nick. Now all he had to do was keep Jude from touring too soon with Max, and bring Robbie around – at least to the point where the other pickers could stop cutting the air, so filled with bad feeling. Sometime soon he'd have to go to the shed, clean it up, and get his stuff. But not yet. There was nothing he needed that Jude didn't have.

He listened to the four of them breathing, the dogs, Jude, himself, out of sync, but filling in each other's spaces like one efficient unit. Jude stirred. 'The dogs are back,' he told her. She sighed and rolled over. Her body fitted into the curve of his own, her belly dwarfed by his hand as he stroked it. He breathed down her spine, lulled by the hissing crackle of wind in the rivergums, like scratches in the grooves of an old record.

Early the next morning she took him to the river. He followed in the wake of her humming, a new song coming, she said. Along the bank he stumbled while Jude leapt across tree roots velvety with dark moss, over rocks hairy with pale lichen. She was following the flow of the river, showing him how the light changed on the surface of the water. It was one of those details he'd always known about, but never really noticed. Now he stopped to watch, this interaction of light and water, so solidly visible, ephemeral and untouchable.

'I dreamed you sold the dogs,' she said eventually.

'Did I get a good price?'

'You sold them to me, you fraud.'

She went back to her humming, and eventually it turned to words, the song becoming clearer to him: *climbing up the happiness chain*. In the light of her story the other night it took on an entirely different meaning. At the bend in the river she said hello to a sapling as if it had been waiting for her. She pulled the young tree to her chest. 'How's it going, Mum,' she murmured.

Perhaps her song wasn't ironic. It might only be a tree, but Nick could see her loving the way the slender trunk sprang back when she let it go, quivering. The sapling was shooting up, but it was still a baby with tender green leaves and silky bark.

'When did she die?'

'A year ago.' Jude's face was remote, but her voice creaked with misery. 'It was a car accident, and it was my fault.' She started walking aimlessly along the river bank and Nick fell into step beside her, trying to keep her to a track as she talked.

𝄞

They'd set out for a drive on a good day. A good day because Leni had woken up and seemed to know who she was. Now that her mother no longer spoke in sentences, Jude had to conjure meaning in other ways, from a brighter burning within her eyes, a slackening of her chin, a brief and mysterious deafness.

That morning, as always, Jude had bathed her gently, ducking from Leni's arm when it lashed out, and stroking her kicking legs. She'd shared her food, with a soundtrack of smalltalk, keeping Leni's senses in the benign present, the day clear and glossy, the rich yellow egg yolk, those cheeky magpies, how fat the olives were this year. Keeping her docile. *George has taught me to drive*, Jude told her, pointing to their old rattler. *I've got my P-plates, Mum. George? Max's dad, a friend of ours*, she told Leni, knowing it was too much information. Don't push, don't remind her that she can't remember, and lucky she can't, because she'd want to know why Bruno had been hiding from her.

Sometimes Jude suspected Leni of playing possum, suspected that she knew Bruno had sold off the olive grove and all they had left now were the two acres this side of the river. Standing at the back of the house, Jude had looked across the river at the trees that were no longer theirs, and cried at Bruno's incompetence. Leni had never asked about them. She never asked why Jude was there during the day when she should have been at school. All Leni asked that day was to be taken for a drive.

'Ga,' she said, jutting her chin in the direction of the track to the road, where the sun was already laying down shadows from the river trees. It'd be just the two of them, out to see the world while Leni still recognised it as her bit of country.

Getting her into the car was as simple as getting her into the bath. Lift her from the wheelchair, turn the body and lower it, a procedure that had become easier as Leni wasted. The hard part was strapping her in, with Leni scratching at Jude's fingers to stop her fiddling with the clunky old seatbelt. They'd set off, Jude reversing over Leni's campfire, winding through the trees to the road and Leni's beloved plain where the crows lived. Past the garage and into Crundle, past the scribbly gums this side of town and up the main street with the mulberries sprouting fresh new leaves, and the wattles thinking about flowering; past Harry's Feed Store, Frank and Sue's newsagent and Shirley's Hardware, glancing all the time at Leni in case something surfaced on that blank profile. A blink would have done. Turning at the garage on the other side of town, grinding the gears exactly the way George said not to, and out of town in a flash. Back on the open road, pointing to the stray cows, the way home. And Leni getting twitchy at the mention of home, her gulping throat, and her fingers plucking at the air in her lap.

Leni's arm, which should have been weak, flung open the door with a strength she must have been storing up by not speaking, not moving, not loving. She turned her head, taking a look at the daughter who had washed and cursed her and come to the hospital to sleep by her bed, and brought her home and dressed and fed her, and played music and sung to her for eight years. Leni's frightened eyes said that she'd known Jude would come up with a way, eventually. That this was her last chance to jump ship before it sank.

𝄞

Jude stopped, her hair falling over her face as she cried softly. Nick waited, knowing not to speak, afraid to touch her. 'The seatbelt didn't click in,' she said eventually. 'It would have taken her the whole trip into town to get her arm out from under it. And I didn't lock the door, didn't think of it. She couldn't have done it if the door was locked. And I keep wondering whether she expected the door to be locked, that I was supposed to have made it harder for her.'

'How would she know if she was senile?'

'She was never senile – it was a disease,' she said, nearly choking as she gulped in air. 'Huntington's Disease.'

He'd never heard of it. But he'd never asked if Leni was senile either, had just assumed it from the story. The townspeople would have wondered whether Jude could have made it harder for her mother, and so would've Bruno. So did Nick. He also wondered if he'd want to stay alive with a disease like that, one that dismantled your body and mind by instalments, just so you knew what you were in for. Nick squeezed her fingers. *What do you say when there's nothing you can say to make it better?*

'Everyone knows, don't they?' he said.

'It's not something you can hide.'

'Is that why people in the pub are a bit reserved with you?'

The look she cast him was confounded. 'Reserved? I always thought they were sorry . . .'

'I guess that's what I meant – I mean, I didn't know what it was until now.'

She picked up a stone and lobbed it into the bush. 'I've got to get ready for work. So do you.'

𝄞

On the way back to the house they came across Bruno gazing across the water at his lost trees. 'What he's going to tell you,' Jude whispered as they approached, 'is that he never intended to be an olive farmer, but the trees were there and he wept at the sight of them and felt that he'd come home, even though there weren't any where he came from, and he had no idea how to farm them, and never learnt. You've got to listen. I can't anymore.' She left him with Bruno and went to feed the dogs.

'A lot of people used to come here, oh yes,' Bruno said after the olive-farming story. 'Songs and campfires for nearly half the year. But not now.'

'What happened?' Nick asked politely, expecting Bruno's version of the Leni story.

'Only the passage of time happened.'

Nick towered over Bruno as they surveyed the olive grove across the water, both of them standing with legs apart and arms folded across their chests. Being blokes, he supposed.

'You know what I use to do, back in Budapest?' Bruno didn't wait for an answer. 'I work in the eye clinic. I took photos of people's eyes. You take pictures of enough eyes, look into enough eyes, and have enough eyes look back at you, and you find out they don't say nussing, no soul living back there, only a lump of brain. You look into enough people's eyes and you find out all what counts is not hiding, is out here where you can see it.'

Reading the bewilderment in Bruno's eyes, Nick was unconvinced.

'He's strong on theory,' Jude said, arriving with the dogs leaping around her.

The look Bruno gave her filled Nick with pity. He thought

Jude shrank from it, too. 'Why do you hate him?' he asked her, watching Bruno stumble on the step into the house.

'Because he deserted us.'

'But he didn't leave.'

'I don't think you understand desertion.' The sudden formality of her tone nearly crushed him.

'And there's the other reason,' she went on. 'He thinks I murdered Leni. He's never said it, but he does. He's too afraid to ask if I did it deliberately. I ask it all the time, because I knew she wanted to die, and so did Bruno. There was an inquest and I wasn't held at fault. That's the truth, but he won't face it.' Her face was laid open with misery. She began to walk away, then turned to take his hand, filling him with guilt at his sudden longing for the sparkly Jude with the tender smile he'd first met.

'Maybe she trusted you to leave the door unlocked.'

Her sigh was low and fragile as she took his hand and pressed it to her.

'What can I do?' he asked her.

'Just be true.'

'I am, I will be,' he gushed, wondering what exactly being true meant when Jude was saying it.

14

They put Al on a drip. Then they put a feeding tube down his throat, and then they moved him out. That morning Lindy and her company were sitting around him, doing their thing, gossiping, complaining, filling him in on the ebb and flow of life in their ward. They always knew when to pull the sheet over, and they did so before they left. He looked like normal Al, the body under the sheet, and his little sigh could have been just a bit of wind, so Lindy didn't notice for a while that he'd passed out.

Nick's sty was back, stinging at the sight of the vacant bed. All those times he'd joined Al on the ceiling, searching for new cracks. They could have talked about that, what the cracks meant. Loss, unexpected and sharp, hit him for not talking more, and guilt put the boot in for giving up. Too late, he wondered what Al was feeling. *The things you don't say can be as bad as the things you do.*

Lindy came to clear Al's locker, shrieking for her whips

and planets, pulling out threadbare singlets and pyjama pants, shaking out chocolates from the folds. The woman was a giant; she could have saved Al from starvation with those chocolates, pushed them into his mouth and sat on him till they went down, instead of shovelling them into her own gob. She glanced over to Nick. For a second the eyes behind the pharaoh eyeliner were grief-stricken.

'He's starving and dehydrated,' she said. 'But he won't die, poor Al.'

'Does he want to die?'

'No. He wouldn't worry about his food being poisoned if he wanted to die.'

The locker was emptied and Al's paltry clothes were stacked on the stripped mattress. Lindy came to Nick's bedside and sat on the chair, arranging her purse, her skirt, and carefully pushing back strands of hair from her face. 'He had a brain tumour once. They took it out and said he was cured, but he never believed them. He's afraid of it coming back.'

'But why does he worry about his food being poisoned?'

'He thinks whoever gave him the tumour wants him dead. He thinks the contaminated food will make it grow. Sticking to white food's pretty smart, if you ask me.'

'It's crazy.'

'Not as crazy as you thinking it's crazy,' she said. 'He's got a system. He's got this map of his brain in his head, but he projects it onto the ceiling because it's easier to see up there, and he keeps track of which path a tumour might take.'

'He's not counting cracks in the ceiling?'

'Why would he do a useless thing like that?'

Nick had a sudden coughing fit. 'Have they done tests?'

'Yes, and they said there's nothing there, but why should Al believe them?'

'So he's going to die of an imaginary tumour.'

'But it might be real, it might come back.' Lindy said. 'And his food might be poisoned.'

Nick thought of Jude, living with her fear, not imaginary, but possibly non-eventuating. Jude was waiting for the passage of time, but that hadn't stopped her from cramming the tunnel with her fragile hopes and her wonderful, extravagant, voice.

'You must love him, talking to him all the time. It must be frustrating never getting an answer.'

'It's not frustrating, but I don't love him, not like I love Mark . . .'

'Why do you love Mark?' Nick broke in. The guy was a turd. 'He's . . .'

'Because he lets me do his hair,' she said quickly, then leaned over to add confidingly, 'I don't love him as much as I love my doctor, though.' She straightened up. 'Al's not even a friend, really – he used to be a truck driver, so he was hardly ever in town. But he's from our ward. I only do small things. Mainly, I be there for him. And his locker is a good place to store chocolates.'

Nick expelled a long breath. Small things. Being unafraid of being there while Jude waited for the passage of time. 'Don't you feel trapped sometimes?'

'No.' She got up and went over to Eric, who had his head buried in a magazine. 'Can I have the *Who*? Iris told me there was a whole section on hairstyles in it. I'm going to test one on Mark.'

'All right, Lindy love, but bring it back,' he said, handing it over, and flashing a gold-toothed smirk at Nick. 'Nick hasn't read it yet. And can you get me another one?' She gave him one from the pile on the locker; he lay back on the pillows and opened it over his face. She gathered up Al's belongings.

'I reckon there won't be any birthday party, then,' Nick said. Lindy answered with a huffy grunt and proceeded to the doorway, where she forced Nurse Sunni to stand aside as she made her exit. 'Say hi to Trace,' Nick called out, but whether she heard he didn't know.

Nurse Sunni entered then with a dressing tray, and Nick prepared to meet her with his usual resistance to whatever she wanted to do to him.

'What?' he said.

'Your sty.'

He'd forgotten it. He checked the clock while Nurse Sunni put the tray on his locker, but it was hours before Iris and her gold wedding band were due. Breathing in her familiar disinfected smell as she lightly dabbed on some stinging substance with a hand that had no ring weighing it down, he said, 'Aren't you engaged, Nurse Sunni?'

'Not now.' She sent Nick a smile, so sudden and so winning, that he beamed one back.

'Well . . . congratulations, I suppose.'

'Thanks, it's a relief.' Nurse Sunni's new confiding tone was making his heart melt. At last she was talking to him like a person. 'A mistake, marrying into that family,' she went on. 'I'm like you, from out of town, and no matter how long I live here I'm always going to be a blow-in to them.'

'You know,' he said, 'a pile of stuff went wrong for me in Crundle, but nobody ever made me feel like a blow-in.' The realisation was as sudden and unexpected as Nurse Sunni's smile had been. All she did now was nod and he didn't pursue it because he didn't want to get into an argument; all he wanted was to soak up Nurse Sunni's unforseen rush of warmth. 'But then, I wasn't going to marry anybody. Poor Nurse Sunni,' he said. 'Are you going to leave town?'

She gave a rusty ting of a laugh, and packed up the dressing tray. 'Of course not! I'm going to get engaged to a man from another local family.'

They both laughed, but Nick was perplexed. Eric pulled the magazine off his face. 'Blow-ins are forgiven a lot more than locals,' he said to Nurse Sunni, and then waved to Lindy who'd appeared at the door again. 'That's the pay-off.'

'Hey Nick,' Lindy said.

Nurse Sunni's body resumed its usual rigidity. She pointed at Lindy's stilettos. 'Look at those dreadful shoes, pock-marking the floor,' she said. 'Al's gone, Lindy, and you are no longer a valid visitor. Nor are your cronies. So leave now.'

Lindy ignored her. 'Hey Nick,' she said again.

Nick looked from her to Nurse Sunni and back to Lindy, who had a regality that transcended her size. It was a stand-off between them both and neither had to work at being imposing.

'We're going to have the party anyway,' Lindy said to Nick. 'We decided to have it at your place – your bed.'

'No, you're not.' Nurse Sunni told her. She turned her intensifying smile onto Nick.

All this new warm and fuzzy with Nurse Sunni, stuff he'd been craving, that Nurse Sunni would treat him like a person, would make him feel *valid*. Nick gave a silent groan. Eric's bed creaked and rattled as he pulled himself up higher on the pillows, his bloodshot eyes glowing, more perky than he'd ever been.

'I'm a valid visitor,' Lindy said quietly.

Nurse Sunni gave a dry laugh.

'She is,' Nick said to Nurse Sunni. 'She's my visitor.'

'Mine, too,' Eric chipped in.

With icy dignity, without another word or look, Nurse Sunni left.

'It'll be a practice party,' Lindy said to them. 'So we get it right when Al comes back.' She edged up to Nick, her voice all soft and breathy as she held out a small bar of chocolate.

'Would you like a Whip?'

'Gee, thanks, Lindy.'

She unwrapped it for him, and he smiled when he saw the wrapper, always so carefully stuffed into her little black purse: Cadbury's Caramel Whip. She broke off a square and popped it into his waiting mouth. She hesitated, then held out another, a mini Mars bar. 'Would you like a planet, too?'

'I'll save it for when I can unwrap it myself.'

She put it in his locker drawer. 'See you tomorrow.'

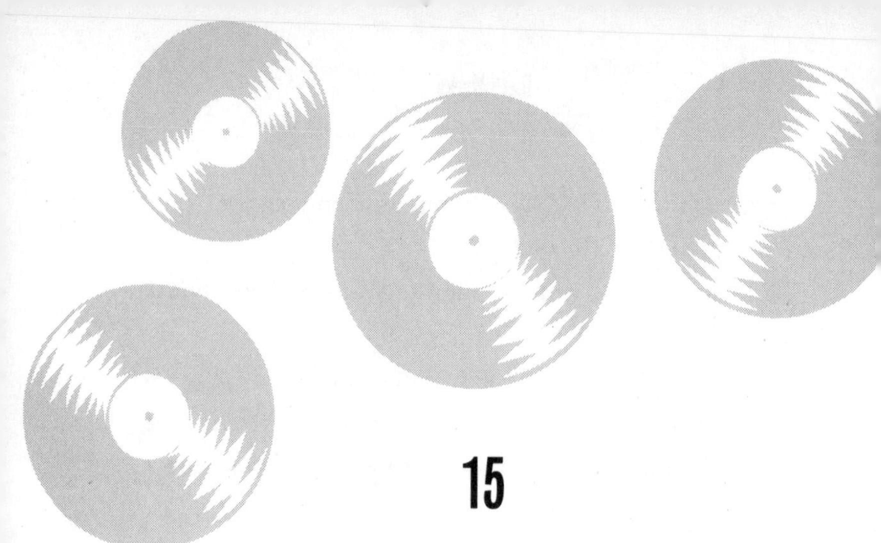

15

'IT'S ONLY NERVES,' JUDE REMINDED HIM AT THE FAT STAG, when Nick complained that the lights were too bright. It was another Wednesday and they'd come in the Rodeo with Max. Nick had tied the dogs to the verandah post, leaving Jude to go and talk to the band. 'I'll tell Steve what song you're doing,' she told him. He'd nodded nervously, avoiding Max's smug smile.

'Don't worry,' Max said to him as he slouched away with Jude. 'The band's tight, you can't stuff them up.'

A girl Nick had never seen before was already up and singing. She wasn't too bad, not too good, and the audience was the usual bunch, they weren't hostile. Unlike Robbie, who cast him one of his dismissive sneers and turned back to talk to the guy with the bear-claw rings. Nick went up to him anyway. He'd never found out the guy's name, but there was Robbie, calling him Dave and dispensing advice on how to get himself a new image.

'Shoes, mate, the first thing girls look at. Get some spectacular shoes, and you'll slay 'em.'

Dave Bear-claw nodded as earnestly as his goofy smile would let him, soaking up Robbie's wisdom. Nick remembered the girl in the green pedal pushers. Maybe Dave would pay attention.

'He made me buy these snazzy boots,' Nick said, lifting a foot.

'And did they ever work,' Robbie said, staring at the black bruise line under Nick's eye. 'Because he's got nothing else going for him.'

'Yep, snagged the girl and they're not even broken in yet,' Nick said, playing cool like Robbie used to. 'I'm singing tonight,' he told them.

'Great,' Dave Bear-claw said. 'These talent shows are a hoot, eh?'

Robbie leaned against the bar, raised his eyebrows and sipped his beer.

'Where's Angie?' Nick asked.

'On her way back to Dublin,' he said absently.

Jude joined them with a cheery hello to Robbie before turning to Dave Bear-claw, calling him Davy, telling him how a beer would soften and soothe her vocal cords. She turned back to Robbie and they laughed about the miracle of her house not being burnt to the ground yet, now that Nick was there. Jude winked at Nick, oblivious to Robbie's cool smile.

They both watched her cut a swathe through the crowd to the toilet, to do whatever it was she did in there before gigs. He never asked; it was something private, one of the many private things about her. But he needed something too, to soothe his throat, to distract him from the way Jude had been so attentive to Robbie, which reason and experience told him could be put down to mild guilt about bonking your old mate's mate. He needed distraction from the way Robbie regarded the exposed flesh of Jude's legs, the skin between the tops of her boots and the swinging fringe of her spangly cowgirl skirt. He felt bile rising. *Keep your eyes off her arse*, he wanted to say. *Off everything. Look away.* This stupid fear when he knew everyone checked out other people's bodies. It didn't mean they wanted to bonk them. Well, it probably did, but it didn't mean they'd do it. He eyed Robbie. *Would he?*

'She looks happy, doesn't she,' Nick said.

Robbie grunted. 'She tell you the rest of the story?'

'She did.' When Robbie kept staring at him, Nick said, 'Why don't you tell it your way, then?'

'It's not my story.'

'That's never stopped you before.'

'Ouch,' Robbie said with his cool smile. 'Keeping your claws sharp, aren't you? You must be – two weeks in the wilds and the dogs haven't eaten you yet.'

Just then Jude emerged and the band called her up. She blew Nick a kiss on her way to the microphone. He relapsed into being a bunch of nerves, barely hearing her sing, just waiting for her to call him on stage and seeing himself tripping over on the way, forgetting the words, forgetting what vocal cords were meant for. In the corner the guy at the mixing desk was keeping Jude's voice clear and free, not letting it drown under the instruments. He hoped the guy would take the same care with his voice, which needed it so much more. The sound guy looked up, caught Nick's anxiety, and gave him a hand signal, which could have meant either 'no worries' or 'you're stuffed'.

When Jude's set was over the air felt thinner. He inhaled great gulps of it, as if he were on top of some alpine monster. He didn't hear Jude call him up through the rush of blood in his ears, though he knew she must have, because now she was beckoning him, and somebody – it must have been Dave Bear-claw – shoved him forward. Lurching towards the band, he imagined their disdain; they were waiting for him to get on with it, get out of the way so that Harry from the Feed Store could do his number. As if praying, the guitarists' heads were bowed over their instruments. Nick took hold of the microphone with reverence as his heart fluttered in double time to Steve's string-slapping. Steve smiled a half smile, his eyes droopy as he hit the strings with big floppy pats, like a drowsy tiger that knows exactly how sharp its claws are. Nick was up on the stage, all of six inches above the crowd, looking down at too many pink shirts and silver shoes and Robbie's slicked hair. His teenage fantasy had materialised, and he wished he'd never been near Cliff's shed, never listened to Roy.

He was singing 'Blue Moon', the easy, melodic one; the one he couldn't stuff up. It was only one song, and all he had to do was get through it.

He opened his mouth, and he was flat.

'A,' Steve said. 'Get into A.'

Is he talking to me, Nick wondered, *or the guitarist?* He didn't know where A was. Up? Down? Jude had told him things about A, but he couldn't remember what. The guitarists repeated the opening riffs placidly, as if it was nothing to them whether he sang or not. Then Frank and Sue, decked out in matching red shirts and toothy encouragement, moved to the front and gave him the thumbs up. He turned to Jude, grateful she was still on stage, sitting it out on a guitar case beside the drummer. She nodded for him to carry on, and so he began again.

Whenever he tried to recall this, the opening moment of his big break, Nick could only remember a feeling of mild panic. More like standing in a tub of molasses than sinking in quicksand. He hadn't thought his breath would be so shortened by nerves, but Jude had known and he'd always thank her for the breathing lessons. He heard his voice, shaky, too thin, but holding the tune. The original words were imprinted on his brain, but what came out was, *Blue moon, you saw my heart on its knees.* The words might be wrong, but now he felt it under his skin, a song of joy, of relief and gratitude, and it seemed to him as he moved further into it that he sang with a new set of vocal cords. People picked up on his feeling, and started swaying a little with the undulating melody; they weren't the crowd any longer, they were on his side, locals who'd all been up here at one time or another. Turning to face Jude he sang, *I saw my dreams spread before her.* And for a moment he was filled with hope that this was it, that singing was their common thread, their common chord. Her smile was a little pained as he tried to hit a top note he never could get, this time with a bit of sigh the way she'd shown him. He missed it again, his voice cracking into a feeble squeak, and the crowd cheered.

Robbie came over with the other Irish backpacker, Enya. He shook his head happily. 'Man, you were so bad.' He slapped Nick on the shoulder, then swaggered off with his arm around Enya. Guess that's one way to get your mate back.

'You'll never match her.'

It was Max, whispering in his ear as Nick passed him in a daze of relief and strange elation. 'You know that, don't you?'

Nick didn't grasp what he was saying, could only grin stupidly at him, and then Jude was there, all sparkly, giving him a Coke and one of her sweet long kisses.

'So I didn't completely bomb?'

'You can't bomb here,' she said. 'You were wonderful.'

𝄞

Max drove while Nick and Jude sat in the back of the Rodeo. Going down the hill they passed Beulah's Books where Nick saw that the bloke who'd been sleeping in the doorway had got himself a new stack of cartons and was arranging them for his bed. How did you get that down and out in a town as small as this? he wondered, relieved he could slip by with his arm around Jude and avert his eyes, because he didn't want to know the details of failure.

'Nobody knows who he is,' Jude said as they continued their descent and the bloke sank into the night. 'He just showed up a couple of months ago and set up house. He doesn't bother anyone and so far nobody's bothered him.'

'So he's no relation to Beulah?'

'Probably not. Beulah was Frank and Sue's dog. They went broke up there, so they moved down and took over the newsagent. But this guy,' she said, 'I think he's there because it's a homely shopfront.' She struggled in the warm wind to wrap up her hair in her bandanna. 'Somebody in town will find out who he is. They always do.'

The wind stayed warm as Max drove them across the plain. It had become a routine, hopping in the back with the bike in the mornings, and riding from the turn-off where Max dropped him. The Rodeo was a two-seater, and he could have asked Jude to sit with him, but he didn't want to test Max's breaking point. But on Wednesday evenings they rode home in the back together, and tonight they watched the night swallow their tracks.

At some indeterminate point of the road Jude changed. Her body didn't stiffen, but he felt her shift, on guard now. There was nothing he could say about it because there was nothing defined, nothing measurable or visible. He thought it must be the place where Leni jumped, that they'd passed through some permanent disturbance in the ground, the border between the sparkly and the dark Jude. Soon the wind turned against them with stinging whips so they hunkered down, tracking the clouds rolling across the moon.

'There'll be a storm tonight,' Jude said drowsily. 'We'll have to stay in the house.'

𝄞

The rain had stopped when he woke in the night. Listening for Jude's breath, all he heard were leaves rustling and frogs groaning in their sleep. Then he saw her standing before the mirror. Bright white moonlight, like a celestial gauze bandage, was unravelling through the window. Naked, she was standing to attention, and he lay watching as she held up her hands and examined their reflection in the mirror, as if she didn't want to see them too clearly.

'What are you doing?' he asked, sitting up. She froze.

'Testing for nerves.' She sounded ashamed. 'For steadiness.'

Even he could see that her fingers were so motionless they could have been asleep. She picked her way over the extension cords, speakers and guitars to the bed. 'You haven't told me the whole story, have you?' he said. 'Everybody seems to know it except me.'

'I'm sorry, I was squeezing every drop of your sunny ignorance, prolonging the normality.' She crawled under the sheet and he untangled her long hair, freeing the back of her neck from its heat and weight.

'It took so long to find out what was wrong with Leni. Even now I can't tell when it started, just a bad temper every now and then for no special reason, and we'd hardly notice it, or we'd put it down to a mood. Sometime later she began to forget what to do in which order – I'd go outside and there she was pegging the clothes out on the line, only she hadn't washed them yet.

'Max found the dogs around that time – they were just puppies, dumped by the river, and he thought Leni would like them. I took them in to show her and she was like a kid, wanting to pat them. But her leg went out of control and kicked Biff in the head. So they'd never go near her. "They tremble at the sight of me," she'd say. I told her it was the breed, they were whippets, high-strung, and she said, "I know what bloody breed they are!"' Jude's drawling imitation of her mother turned Leni into someone Nick could recognise – she sounded like Maree. 'It was so funny when she said that,' Jude went on. 'She was so pissed off at me. Now, I can see it was one of the last times she said a whole sentence. They wouldn't go near her, but she really loved those dogs.

'And then her hands went like a puppet's. They'd jerk in all the wrong directions, as though she was being controlled by some crazed puppeteer. That's when Bruno got frightened and took her to the hospital in Marston. And when we did find out, we couldn't do anything about it, just care for her as best we could.' She held up a hand and wriggled her fingers until Nick took it in his own and lay it across his chest.

'An inherited disorder of the brain, the doctor said. No cure, and half a chance that I will get it. Symptoms start around thirty.'

Nick wanted to cry for her.

'You know,' she said, 'you can't believe it, that you can't *do* anything – pain relief was the only treatment, and the rest was just to love her. I screamed about it and Bruno screamed at me: "Nussing to do about it, nussing to do but wait."' She mimicked Bruno's voice with an eerie perfection. 'Then he'd scream at Leni: "You Vegemites, only care what's there on the end of your nose, no stories, never keeping track of your own people. Never knew who was your people, never asked." He couldn't take it then, and he still can't. All he did was kill time wandering in the olive grove. Leni used to keep a grip on him and without her his sense just drifted.'

There was a test, but Jude refused to take it.

'I told you, there's no cure. I don't want to know about it if there's no cure.' She tested herself, she said, tested her hands in front of the pub toilet mirror, before her gigs.

'Yeah, I've seen you do it. Some test.' And what he'd thought was a lovely habit, the way she looked at her hands when she spoke, was probably another test.

'The doctors say it's meaningless, but it's my only gauge, it's what I can see, and it helps keep the panic down.'

He wanted to cry for her, and he wanted to make her feel better. Exactly how inheritable was an inheritable disease? Half a chance was fifty per cent. Symptoms at thirty.

'Who'd want to live past thirty?' he said with a studied flippancy.

'I would.'

Nick found himself nodding knowingly when he didn't know at all. He lay there feeling like he'd been slugged. It had been the Leni story before, but now it was personal.

'You've got ten years before you're thirty,' he said, as if she didn't already know. 'That's forever. Didn't they teach you to have faith in science?'

'Nope – didn't get as far as faith.' She grabbed his hand. 'Nice to have an optimist around, though. Max gets nervous if I trip over something, thinks it's a sign.'

Max again. *Wears a heart up his sleeve like a dirty trick.* For a moment Nick was deaf with jealousy and the threat of being up against another mate, this one full-time and permanent. When he listened again Jude was still talking.

'When I hit thirty I'll wake up every day checking that

I haven't pegged dirty clothes on the line. I'll be in suspense until I'm fifty. By then I'll be exhausted and probably want to die.'

'No you won't. I won't let you.'

'Then *you'd* be exhausted.'

'You're making it so hard.'

'Other people are sorry for me. I didn't want you to be. When you arrived that first night, you were so easy – you didn't know me. Robbie didn't know much, at least not when he arrived. It would have been easier not to tell you, but I had to, or somebody else would have.'

Not Robbie, though. Robbie was true.

16

There was a new person in Bert Jawframe's bed. His name was Bob Jawframe. It was an effort for Nick to refrain from asking about occupational hazards. Bob's wife had entered with their child, who immediately climbed onto the bed and made a grab for her father's metal halo. As dull as Bert's, it was probably the same halo.

'Not Daddy's sick bits, Sophie,' the mother gently chided, unclenching grasping fingers.

When she lifted Sophie off the bed, the child clutched at the sheets and plucked at the hairs on Bob's exposed legs. Bob's eyes fluttered with pain, but his wife laughed and gave Sophie the car keys to play with. You could tell by Sophie's almost-smile that she'd added something to the list of things she could get away with. Nick knew that smile, though it had been a while since he'd used it. He watched Bob's wife, sitting on the edge of the visitor's chair, desperately grabbing at random chat items, the way visitors did with their outsider fear. Even husbands and wives.

'The nurses might wish you were dead sometimes,' Eric murmured to him, 'but they're the only ones who treat you like you're still alive.' He stole a look at the clock, but it was still only three o'clock. 'Except the wife,' he conceded. 'She's used to it, me being in and out of here. Gives her an interest, being around other blokes with different ailments.' He stared past Nick, out the window where the sky was a rare regal blue. 'Well, a change, certainly a change.'

'Nick.'

It was Robbie, deftly stepping over Sophie who was emptying a bag of marbles onto the floor. He slumped into Nick's bedside chair as if he was in his own bedroom. Nick opened his mouth to speak, but Robbie was already distracted, this time by Nurse Sunni's brisk entrance into the ward with a bedpan.

'Who's that?' he breathed.

'My personal sadist,' Nick said. 'You've seen her, she was there the night I came in.'

'I don't remember,' he said, watching her pull the curtain round Eric's bed. 'I was distracted by other things that night.'

'You've just got the attention span of a guppy.'

When Nurse Sunni emerged Robbie asked her, 'How's my friend?' He gave Nick's hospital gown a straightening tug at the neck.

'He's been receiving the best care,' said Nurse Sunni, taking no notice of Robbie's smooth smile. 'Of course a lot depends on his *co-operation.*'

Robbie turned to Nick. 'What does she mean by that?' To Nurse Sunni he said, 'He's practically mummified. What kind of co-operation are you talking about?'

'She means I should try harder to piss *into* the bottle, and smile more,' Nick said.

'Tough call,' Robbie said, trying on his lopsided grin to impress her. Nurse Sunni retreated with a cool glance at Nick's pained smile, and only emitted a professional sigh as she slipped on one of Sophie's marbles. Entranced, Robbie watched her cajole Sophie into helping her pick them up, and then deposit them in Bob's locker drawer. Nick decided not to tell him that her immunity to his charms, aside from taste, would be due to her proposed new engagement. When she left, Robbie remembered he was there to visit Nick.

'You're getting a beard there – guess you never got another shave from Dave?'

'I think it was a one-off. Maybe he got insulted that I slept through it. I reckon he should've been flattered.'

'Doesn't that nurse shave you?'

'I wouldn't let her near me with a blade.'

'I'll do it – beats sitting around trying to chew the fat.'

'No, I can wait.' But he was too slow in refusing. Robbie was already on his way out the door, gone in the direction, Nick assumed, of Nurse Sunni. He was back in no time with a steel bowl of slopping hot water, soap, disposable razor and a frayed brush, all on a tray.

'That's country hospitals for you. Haven't seen a brush since my grandpa died. Used to shave him though, so reckon I can remember the drill.'

Clearly relieved to be doing something, he pulled the curtains all the way around the bed, attempting some kind of privacy, which Nick appreciated, but didn't acknowledge. He grabbed the towel from the rail on the locker and draped it across Nick's neck. Nick looked at Robbie's capable gardener's hands and hoped they were steady enough to wield a razor.

Dipping the brush into the water, Robbie rubbed it into the soap, slowing his hand to test the lather as if for years he'd been secretly watching his father make gelato. He worked the soap into Nick's skin with the brush, and Nick succumbed to its soft texture against his cheeks. He closed his eyes in a moment of weakness and when he opened them again the underside of Robbie's chin was suspended above him.

'You need a shave yourself,' he said.

When Robbie leaned in closer to concentrate on the tricky space between lip and nose, his cheeks flopped forward a little, showing where there'd be two little valleys either side of his nose when gravity caught up with him. Nick stared, fascinated by this glimpse into the future. There were a few lines of stilted chatter from Bob Jawframe's wife and some squeaks from Sophie, but the walls of the curtain created a dreamy, shadowy feeling.

'A long time since I've done this.' Robbie picked up the razor. 'Don't worry,' he snickered. 'It's like a bike, you never forget how.'

Nick might have given him a tight smile, but his cheek twitched just then at the touch of the razor. His eyelids fluttered open to get a close-up of Robbie's suddenly huge fingers and the blur of fine black hairs near the knuckles as they hinged around the handle of the blade.

'Keep your eyes shut.'

He pulled and stretched Nick's skin gently, getting under his chin, around the jawbone. The blade strokes were silent; Nick hadn't developed the scrape yet. He stretched his lip over his teeth so that Robbie could get between it and his nose, and he did it without a hitch. Robbie's hand eased so steadily into the hollows in Nick's face that his mouth relaxed and he couldn't ask the things he supposed he should, such as how Robbie was getting on, whether he was making any money, whether the whole trip was worth it. The burning questions were unaskable. Robbie wasn't talking either, he was being a barber, and now he wiped the leftover splotches of soap from Nick's face.

On the other side of the curtain there was a scuffle, something thudding to the floor, somebody giving a choking yelp of pain. It had to be Bob.

'Sophie!' the mother exclaimed. 'What have you done to him?'

'Pack her off to Nuke Med!' That was Eric. Nick could picture him. From the confines of his bed Eric would still manage to loom over Sophie. 'It's a cave under the building,' he hissed. 'And it's controlled by three witches!'

Now he'd set Sophie bawling.

'You're a menace, Eric Mangels, and you always were!' That was the mother snapping. Eric was going to start a riot, but Robbie just stood there wiping his hands on the towel, as if the space outside the curtain didn't figure on his radar. Then the only sounds were sedate footsteps and resistant little feet leaving the room.

'It's getting stuffy in here. Can you open the curtain?' Nick said.

Robbie pulled it back. Everything appeared to be in order. There was Eric looking jolly and waiting to pounce, Bob seemed happy to be single again, so it must have been Sophie bouncing to the floor. Both Robbie and Nick stared pensively at the teddy bear Sophie had forgotten, strung up by the throat and left hanging from the rail at the end of the bed. Robbie turned to Nick.

'It was an accident, wasn't it?'

This was a Robbie that Nick didn't know, the way he was careful not to catch Nick's eye. Well, he wasn't going to make it easy for him.

'What was an accident? The strangled bear?'

'Come on, Nick. Jude . . .'

'Oh, you mean *Jude*. Are you asking if she drove me to suicidal cycling?'

It was the first time he'd seen Robbie flummoxed. 'Not exactly . . . I mean would it have happened if I'd said you could stay at the shed.'

'Ah.' Now Nick nodded slowly. *He doesn't want forgiveness, he wants absolution.* 'You shouldn't take any credit. It was just an accident.' He used to idolise Robbie, and now he didn't. It wasn't a sudden thought, but it was still a shock. When Robbie glanced back Nick didn't try to disguise the criticism in his face. Robbie would forgive him, even if he did expel a breath heavy with exasperation.

'Girlfriends come and go,' he said to Nick. 'It's your mates that stay.'

'So Jude comes and goes, and you get to keep both of us as mates. Does that mean I lose and you win?' When Robbie opened his mouth to speak Nick cut in again. 'What gets me, is one minute you're so cool and out there, and then, like that time you got freaked out by Lindy, you're like some old geezer from the black and white days.'

Robbie spoke gently, as if Nick were a child in need of comfort and instruction. 'I can be both. I am both.'

Nick considered this. 'So can I, then.'

'I don't know if you get a choice.'

'Maybe not, but it sure makes it easier if you can explain things away like that.' Now he was sounding like Eric.

'And it could be that I'm saying, please Nick, take the good with the not-so-good.'

Take the dark with the light. It was that simple, but be damned if he'd say it to Robbie. 'You think it's that simple?'

'Yeah,' Robbie said. 'You?'

'Not yet.'

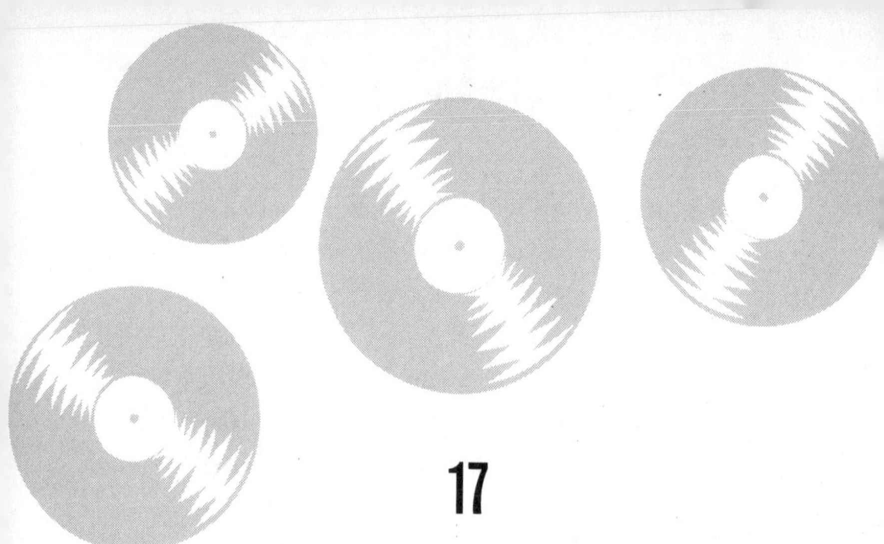

17

THE MOON WAS BRIGHTER THAN LAST NIGHT, AND THE DOGS were baying at it. River smells of mouldy old mud and rotting leaves drifted on the limp breeze and seeped into the mosquito house. Nick and Jude lay on the mat on the floor, while Nick tried to sort things.

'You know,' he ventured, 'there was a moment when I sang in the pub, when the crowd started swaying with me and I thought, *I can do this – I can be a singer.* I was thinking about what you said earlier, about developing your voice . . .' he trailed off, hoping she'd pick up the slack.

'No.'

'If I got good, I could come with you on your tour, we could sing something together . . .'

'Pub bands aren't rich, you know,' she broke in. 'You've got to be a shit-hot singer before they'll take you on without playing an instrument. You've got to earn your keep.'

'But you said I was wonderful.'

The way she looked down, it could have been a nod. 'Oh Nick, you were. But you're not a singer. And you can't play an instrument.'

Her words were like daggers, but he went on. 'If anything happened I could look after you.' He tried to say it casually, but it sounded desperate, his voice creeping about looking for her ear. 'It doesn't have to be this complicated, this hard.'

Her fingers came to rest lightly across his throat. 'I'm not your little brother. If I need help, it'll be much more than steering me home.'

Did she want him to protect her from a meaningless end? Did she want somebody there with an unlocked car door? He couldn't ask, he wasn't that straightforward. 'Jude, I don't know what you want.'

'I want you to be true to me.'

'What does that mean?'

So gradually did her grip tighten that he barely noticed until he suddenly gasped. The snaking movement of her leg might have been a trick of the moon, just a ghostly limb, until her foot found his pelvis and began to grind. Her foot was cool, the grind measured. Here it comes, after all these years, the rest of the body is following the ghostly fingers. Like a rabbit caught in a spotlight he was mesmerised, watching her descend on him, her head lowering to his belly, he watched her bite him, felt the sting of broken skin, the heat of his blood on her tongue when she kissed him. He strained to kiss her back, because he thought he loved her and because that's what his cock was telling him to do. They rolled off the mat, he lay beneath her on the packed-earth floor. It was getting slippery with their sweat. He kicked out, not knowing if it was in pain or desire, but his foot only connected with the mesh wall.

She was unzipping him. *Help her a little.* When she sat on him he didn't have her, she had him. Her teeth in the moonlight were gleaming knives. His eyes, puddled with sweat, were burning. She was on his back, her nails down his spine ripping troughs for their sweat to glide down. His body had a mind of its own, didn't have to be forced into anything. He heard the mesh wall rip.

'This is me.' Her teeth were coming for him again and he raised himself, lunged for her throat, aiming for blood. All this pleasure, their bodies gliding in each other's salty slipstream, he could take a little pain with it and so could she.

'This is me,' she said again, her face hidden by her hair. 'This is how I am.' She reached out, pulled him back into her. 'You can take a little pain.'

He could have crushed her, but he let her teeth bite home. The dogs were baying at the moon and his own howl joined them. She let his head fall back and smiled.

This is us.

There was something new in her eyes, a whorl of need so deep he couldn't see the end of it, and he recoiled from it.

He nearly cried out at the ache. This time it came from some part of him that he didn't know and had no name for, and it felt as if he'd lost the thing that had just made the world a bearable place, lost it before he knew what it was. There was nothing to do about it, and he couldn't pretend that it hadn't happened.

He left her sleeping, and stumbled down to the river. He eased himself into the murk that soothed and stung with every movement, and floated on his back, his penis breaking the surface of the water. His mighty gun, it'd be cocked for days, but he could take it. When the water began to numb him he pulled himself out and sat on the bank, watching the river slide around the protruding tree bolls that somehow resisted erosion. They'd never wear away. But he might.

Somewhere out there the dogs were still howling, a baying to raise the dead. He turned his head, but there was no light on at the house, Bruno was sleeping through it. Flopping on his back he took a deep breath of murky river air. *What if she did get sick?* Commitment. It might have been what he'd been pleading for, but if the actual word was there he'd blocked it before it could surface and solidify in his mind. A hard word, not one you'd sing along with. The memory of his lunge for her throat scared him. Her smile scared him more. What was that about?

All he wanted was to go back to how it was, nothing too bloody, just sweet.

When he entered the mosquito house, Jude was sitting on the mat. Tenderly she dabbed at his body with his T-shirt, wiping off leaves and mud. All the anger she'd been firing at Bruno, all the need she released through songs in the sanctuary of the pub. That's what it was about. Together they shivered in the early morning chill, while the dogs scratched their way through the tear in the wall.

'I want to be with you,' he said.

'Which me?'

Even as he took the breath, he knew his pause could ruin him. This is what she means by being true. You take the dark with the sparkly. What did he want? The sparkly.

'All of you.' The doubt in his voice was barely a wobble, but he felt her flinch.

𝄞

When he woke again she was gone, and her absence felt like a gash in his heart. How could he have doubted? Outside a mist was clearing while he stumbled up to the house. He listened for voices, but the only sound as he pulled open the wire screen door was the rhythmic chink of metal on stone. Walking down the dim hallway, Nick had a sudden vision of the family, Jude, Leni and Bruno, in that cranky old house treating each other like ghosts. In the kitchen Bruno was slumped at the table, chiselling out another of those fat stone-women to join the rest of the company on the shelf. Maybe he thought the stones were ideal companions. He lay down his chisel. 'Breakfast for you?'

'Jude's out walking,' Nick explained, heading for the sink. 'I just want some water.' He drank it, brackish from the tank and probably full of mosquito eggs, wishing it was a Coke he'd just nipped round to a corner shop for. Where was she?

'Judit went to work,' Bruno said, taking up the chisel. Nick gulped the water down and left the room.

Outside he wandered around clinging to the sting of her bite on his throat, staring blindly at the damp mouldy leaves under his feet. When he looked up he was at the edge of Leni's campfire clearing. He crossed it, leaving a trail of leaf litter over the sacred campfire. He whistled for the dogs, then called them, 'Biff! Boof!' but they'd gone. She'd left him behind and taken the dogs. You'd only need half a brain to write a song about that.

In the afternoon he rode into Crundle. He didn't want to pick tomatoes, didn't want to look at Robbie's smug face, but he couldn't stay at Jude's. Pushing the bike between the river-gums and paperbarks, he was heading for the road, when he stopped to prod a curling tubular thing with his foot. He picked it up. It was a snake skin, just dropped by the feel of it. Soft, grey and translucent like old sticky tape, it was beautiful. He coiled it up and stuffed it into his pocket.

The endless plain was just a plain, unbroken, no hidden depths, and surrounded by horizon. It was too hot, too steamy and there might be a storm later, but for now all disturbance was contained within him. When he wheeled into town the scribbly gums were casting long bedraggled evening shadows, but shops were still open. He went to Shirley's Hardware. Biff and Boof were waiting outside, and he paused to scratch their ears. He pushed open the door, setting the old-fashioned bell ringing.

'I'll have a dozen coffin nails, please,' he said.

'Stop it,' Jude hissed. There was nobody else in the shop, but she made no move to emerge from behind the counter.

'Why didn't you wake me?'

'I couldn't – you were out to it.' Then she announced, 'I'm leaving on the tour.'

He stared at her in disbelief. 'When?'

'In two days.'

'When did you decide that?'

'Last week.'

'I don't believe you.'

'Max has already lined up the gigs,' she went on. 'I'm taking a chance on my singing.'

What she meant was, *I'm not taking it on you.*

'How long?'

'A couple of months,' she said casually, as if it were a weekend.

'Take me with you – I'll be your roadie. Shit, I'll be your tea-lady.'

'No.' She turned her attention towards the doorway, as

if a Hero was cued to enter for the rescue, but nobody materialised. She turned back to him. 'Max does all that.'

He searched her face, wanting to see anger there, something to fight against, plead with. But she only looked sorry for him, and he didn't know how to fight against that.

'You were always going to tour, weren't you?' he said.

'You knew that.'

'And I was always temporary.' They both knew it wasn't true. He'd had a chance; there had been a test and he'd failed it. Now she was looking over his shoulder at somebody entering the shop.

'I'll see you tonight,' she said.

'At home?'

'At the pub,' she said, going over to the man who was examining a fretsaw. 'I'm doing a rehearsal.'

The bell jangled as Nick left the shop. He stooped to scratch behind Biff and Boof's slender ears. Then he went to the phone booth at Frank and Sue's newsagency and called home. Bowie's tinny but confident voice greeted him from the answering machine. Nick didn't leave a message. He hung up and dialled again to hear Bowie once more. After the beep he let the machine record the silence of Crundle. In the last remaining seconds he spoke. 'Did you get the puppy, Bowie? Did you get the spotty runt?' *Don't take the runt. It'll give you grief.*

18

Five o'clock, and Iris started packing her bag, ready to leave. Eric took the magazine she handed him. 'There's a do on tonight, Irie,' he said. 'Lindy's mob, a song or two, so you might want to hang about a bit longer.'

'Yeah, hang about,' Nick said to her.

She came to inspect his sty. 'Poor boy, these things coming back, they're just pimples.'

'Iris, there's this other thing,' he said. 'There's this girl. I want to write her a letter. If you've got some time to fill in . . .'

Iris's eyes glinted. 'I can do that for you, love. It'll be like old times, when I used to do it for Eric, taking his dictation.' She leaned in close to speak off the record. 'And it will pass the time for me – you can only read so many magazines.'

'Maybe you should bring Kafka with you,' Eric said in a loud whisper.

She smiled to herself, ignoring him, and produced a fat yellow pen from her bag. 'We can start now. What have you got?'

'Nothing – I mean I haven't got paper.'

She went to get some, leaving Nick to think about what he had. He didn't want to be like Robbie, content with his contradictions, but he needed something in himself to hold on to. What it was he wasn't sure, but it had something to do with writing to Jude.

Iris returned with a notepad. 'That lovely Nurse Sunni, she tried to give me two of them, but I thought one would do to start with.' She sat down and looked at him with interest, holding the pad up. 'Unless you've been lying here all this time bursting with ideas and words?'

'No.' He read the drug company logo printed at the top of the pad. 'Tranquillity without side effects.' *Who'd want that?*

Iris sat with poised pen.

'Dear Jude,' he said. No point whispering, Eric wasn't as deaf as somebody his age should be. 'The last thing I ever wanted was a party at my bedside. There's some kind of fringe society here and all of them will be sitting on the contraption that holds my leg together. There'll be a sulky guy banging away on his guitar, and there'll be Lindy in her skirt and ripped top and her little black purse full of Whip and planet wrappers. She's a giant Cleopatra. Robbie thinks she's a freak.' Nick stopped. 'Strike that about Robbie.' He went on, 'I'll never see her again when I get out of here. I owe her a lot and I owe a guy called Al, a genius with a map of his brain on the ceiling. There are others. And if I really have to think about it, I like them a lot. Trace remembers you. I'll always owe you. Love Nick.'

Iris looked up when he stopped. 'I'll tidy it up, love, and then where will I send it?'

She'd be miles away, in some smoky pub, singing her heart out and maybe thinking she'd never go back home. 'Send it to The Fat Stag.' Nothing too personal, too painful for her, just a chatty friendly note. When Iris put the pen down, he said, 'I forgot, there's also some lines for a song to put down. "Sink your teeth in my heart . . ."' he began. Iris, a Kafka reader, didn't flinch. The words tumbled out in small bundles. When he'd run out of them, Iris read everything back to him to check she'd got them right. Half-baked, but Jude would know what to do with them, if she decided to use them.

Standing in the doorway, Victor broke into 'Heartbreak Hotel', doing the thin Elvis hip shakes, advancing towards Al's old bed where two glassy pixies, the addicts Doug and Michelle, languished softly and nervously in each other's arms. Mark had seated himself on the edge of Bob Jawframe's bed, strumming the guitar and more or less keeping up with

Victor's frantic pace. Lindy had placed herself in front of Mark, glowering alternately at his silky new locks and Jilly Jackson's smug smile. Jilly Jackson was a dainty, red-haired woman mincing around the room in a big white hat, and Nick loathed her immediately; Lindy had no hope against her.

'That colour, those curls, aren't real,' said Trace, stuffing a handful of chips into his mouth.

'Does it matter,' he said between swallows, 'when she looks so good?'

'It does to Lindy.' Trace grimaced at the feathery doodads on Jilly's hat. 'Lindy wears a lot of make-up, but you're *supposed* to know it's not real. Jilly Jackson cheats. She's always cheated.'

'You know everybody, don't you,' Nick said, looking around. Bob Jawframe was writing something on Nick's writing pad; he held it up for Mark: GET INTO D. Nick smirked, but just then the key Mark was playing in made a definite change, and Victor started singing in tune. Slurping from mugs of tea, provided courtesy of Pat the wardsmaid, Iris and Eric settled in for the kids' show.

'We know everybody, but we don't know you.' Trace sidled closer to the bed and perched herself on its edge. 'What do you do, Nick?'

'Nothing really,' he recited, 'I'm just out of school, waiting for the next thing to happen.' It sounded more like an incantation than an answer.

'Well, what do you want to do?'

'Shit, Trace,' he said with exasperation. 'I don't know!' Victor had broken into 'Heartbreak Hotel' again, this time going for more tremolo, and his voice hiccupped up and down the scale. 'Seems like everybody's got to have a talent or some kind of passion or they're nobody. I'm still looking for something to be . . .' He rolled his eyes at Trace's raised eyebrows. 'Right now, I just want to be somebody who's not sick.'

'You don't like needy people, do you?'

'Why do you say that?' *Is she talking about Jude?*

'You kind of fade out . . .'

'When did I do that?'

'When your friend came . . .' Trace looked uncomfortable, but determined to stand her ground.

'Robbie's the last person in the world to be needy,' Nick said with relief.

'He needed you the other day – and you weren't his friend.'

'You weren't even there, Trace.'

'I was.'

He believed her. A lot went on without him noticing.

'He visits you and brings you books,' Trace said. 'And you didn't tell him your accident wasn't his fault.'

'I did. I told him it was an accident.'

'You told him he shouldn't take any *credit* for it. And you refused to tell him it that it's okay not to be a nice guy all the time. You of all people. You didn't accept him.'

'I do accept him, Trace. Robbie's straightforward – I mean he's got all those contradictions, but he knows what he is, knows what he's good at . . .' Nick trailed off before words like 'envy' and 'inadequacy' slipped out. 'You mean I should be kinder to people,' he said dryly. *You could make up for a few mistakes.*

'Well, yes. It's not as if you have to *look after* them.'

'That's one thing I don't have a talent for.'

Trace sat there, her flimsy bones barely making a dent in the sheet, commanding his attention. 'Some people think everybody's got a talent, even if they never find out what it is.'

'What do you think?'

'I think there's always something you're good at,' she said, 'but sometimes it's not what you want to be good at.'

'Tough, eh? I guess you get over it. Or you settle for being bad at it.'

'Maybe it doesn't matter if you love doing . . .' she held his eye, '. . . whatever it is you do.'

'Depends how far you want to go with it.'

'Would you stop writing songs because you weren't good at it?'

Yeah, a lot goes on without me noticing. 'How do you know I'm not good?'

'I don't. Are you?'

'I don't know, Trace, I've just begun. No, I'm not good.' Nick paused for Victor's finale, a series of 'he-he-he-heart-breaks'. 'Not yet,' he amended. *And if you never got good, would you stop? No.*

Lindy sailed past them and swiped the hat off Jilly Jackson's head, stamping on it as if it were one of Al's contaminating peas.

'Jilly did Mark's hair,' Trace explained.

Jilly's crimson acrylic nails lashed out at Lindy. Lindy brushed her aside like another pea. Over in the corner, Doug and Michelle cowered against the wall, crouched with their arms around each other in protection. Nick found himself gazing at them. They were an island of love, however needy, however addicted; they sheltered each other and they filled him with yearning. Then Jilly let out an alarmingly deep bellow and came back for more. Lindy raised her colossal hand over Jilly's face to push her back. Mark tossed his guitar onto Bob's bed and waded in between them, which impressed Nick no end. Trace stood up, poised, ready to pounce on whoever needed pouncing on. Mark stamped his feet and whined at Lindy, 'I didn't ask her to do it. She *made* me!'

Nick, with a vision of Mark being forced to submit to hair curlers, laughed out loud. Everyone turned their most disapproving frown on him. Even Doug and Michelle gave him a pair of flinty looks. Even Eric, even Iris. Only Bob

Jawframe remained impassive, but he didn't count; his painkillers had kicked in and he'd fallen asleep. Bob's snuffly snores filled the sudden silence as Nick gaped at them. You're a blow-in, remember. They'll forgive you. Still, it hurt.

'Sorry, I didn't mean to laugh, I meant to cough.'

Lindy grunted and picked up Jilly's hat. 'Did you force him?' she gasped at her. Jilly gave Mark a baleful look and nodded. 'That's all right, then.' Lindy plonked the hat on Jilly's head. Mark expelled the breath he'd been holding and retrieved his guitar from the floor where Bob had kicked it in his sleep.

Then Trace was back at Nick's side, a sparrow twittering in his ear. 'I've got Jilly's mobile. We'll call your little brother,' she said, as if that settled it.

'Can you get a signal here?'

'Of course,' Trace said. 'We're in the big smoke.'

He gave her the number, idly wondering whether his phone was still buried under a sack of wheat.

'Hiya, Bowie.'

'Nick? Nick? Where are you? What's that noise?'

'I'm at a party. That's a guy doing a country version of "Heartbreak Hotel".' Bowie's excited voice down the line made him homesick. 'I called a while ago, but nobody was home. Did you get my email? What did I say? I forgot.'

'About the sheep. That's so cool, shearing sheep!'

Bloody Robbie. 'Yeah, I'll show you sometime. Did you get the runty puppy?' *Let him take the runty one, let him love it.*

'I went back for it and somebody already took it. So I got another one, his name's Jack and I love him and I think Lois likes him because she lets him chew her tail. But I really wanted that spotty one.'

'You'll get over it, and don't worry – whoever took him will love him.'

'Yeah. And I've been going to Time Warp . . .'

'Who's taking you?'

'I've got this cool compass . . .' Bowie faded in and out as Trace lost concentration, let the phone drift from his ear, then held it close again. 'Nick? I always knew the way.'

'Yeah, I know you did.'

'And Mum said she's coming to get you on the twenty-third.'

'What?' His shriek made Trace pull the phone away in a panic. 'Put it back quick,' he hissed at her.

'. . . you asked her to,' Bowie was saying. 'How come you're living at a hospital?'

Bloody, bloody Robbie.

At that moment Jilly Jackson swooped down and snatched the phone away from Trace. 'Not nice,' she said, turning it off. She walked away, leaving Nick with the terrible relief of not having to deal with the outside world for another day.

19

The last thing Nick should have wanted to do was go and watch Jude sing, continue the run of humiliation by showing up because she'd said he could. But here he was, struggling up the hill on the bike to The Fat Stag. He could have left it at the bottom, but the bike was insurance; it wouldn't look as if he'd come hoping she'd take him home with her. Halfway up he gave in, got off and walked the bike. At Beulah's Books the homeless bloke was still sleeping under his cartons. Maybe he didn't prefer the street; maybe there just weren't enough beds to go round. Nick stopped, pulled out the snakeskin from his pocket, and left it on the ground by the bloke's head. He'd like that, a piece of nature to wake up to.

He heaved his way to the top and there, tied to the pole outside the pub, sat Boof and Biff the twin whippets. They jumped up smiling, licking his hand while he chained the bike to their pole. He lingered, ridiculously elated that they remembered him, even if it was only a few hours since he'd seen them outside Shirley's. It had to be a good omen. Being on the ground together had made them amenable to each other – he, who'd never much liked dogs, who'd only ever put up with Lois because she was family.

Who'll look after them if Jude gets sick?

Winding his way through the crowd, he found her at the bar, looking like she hadn't worked all day, but had just woken from a refreshing sleep and ambled over here to stretch the golden vocals. He edged his way over to her and she kissed him lightly on the forehead, like a big sister. She kissed him as if he'd come back from an errand across the road. And it was almost enough.

She flashed him her familiar thin smile. *She's cool, cold even* – but you could be that way when you saved all the emotion for the song. He lowered his voice and ordered a schooner of bitter. 'Softens the old vocals,' he said to her raised eyebrow. Somebody grabbed him by the shoulder.

'In from the wilds, eh?' It was Robbie. He gave Jude a big-brother kiss and watched her walk away. 'What's up?' he said, turning back to Nick.

'Not a lot.'

Irish Enya arrived and threw her arms around Robbie. 'Back to the bad old days, eh?' Robbie said to Nick. His sly grin made Nick want to give him an affable slap on the back. He was so . . . normal.

'There's still hope – but can I camp at the shed tonight?'

Understanding, pity, and vindication crossed Robbie's face in that order. 'Shit, mate, I'm sorry,' he said, casting a glance at Enya. 'It's a bit awkward tonight . . .'

'Don't worry . . . maybe I'll bunk on Tony's porch.' He almost laughed at the bitter theme of a song that came to him: *lose the girl and get your mate back.* He ordered another beer.

Steve plucked at his bass and the drummer did a start-up roll. Nick downed the beer in a couple of gulps. He burped his soured breath into the empty glass, went over to Jude and grabbed her hand. 'You go slay 'em.' Robbie gave her the thumbs up as she took the microphone, and Nick nodded at her soberly. When she broke into 'Take These Chains from My Heart' he felt sick. There'd be pleadings now.

𝄞

'I could still come with you,' he pleaded. 'It's not like I've got any ties.'

Her set was over. They were outside cooling off by the pole the dogs were tied to. There should have been a storm, but the sky was as clear as Jude's eyes once were. The beer had made him fuzzy, and he was fumbling with the dogs' leads, untying them because their whimpers were clearly asking him to. They moved over and sat like stabilisers at either side of Jude's feet. He needed them more than she did.

'It's not like we're finished,' he pleaded. 'I only want you to forgive me – I'm sorry about last night.' He bent to pat Biff, astounded when he suddenly knew it wasn't Boof. 'You know, it's just that you were so sparkly before . . . when I first met you.'

'You were mistaken. That was one moment, and it was all you decided to see.' There was a burst of noise as the swinging saloon doors spat out a group of people. Jude watched them lurch towards the car park, and then turned back to him. 'I've got nothing to lose, I'll sing every song like it's my last.'

All that pain he'd let her give him, that he'd helped her give him. Now he thought he understood why she didn't mind that her clothes, that the house she lived in and that the people around her were all falling apart. She didn't want her things to outlive her. 'All this heartache you're giving me,' he said, 'and I still can't sing like Roy Orbison.'

'You don't know what heartache is,' she said.

They stared at each other, full of grievances. He'd meant it to sound like a joke, but it wasn't, and it didn't sound like one.

Then she said, 'I'm finding my voice, Nick. You helped with that.' Her eyes were unguarded, her voice was silky with the promise of relenting, of second thoughts, of wonder. 'There were times, I was just delirious with you . . .' Perhaps searching for words, she looked down at her hands. So did he. In their steadiness he saw a lifetime of raging need and found himself touching her bite on his throat. When she looked up she caught him staring down at them.

If there was fear on his face it was just another one of those wobbles. But it was as good as abandoning her. He felt her contempt like a slap. Then her eyes were shutting down, dark curtains drawn across the whorls of need.

'No matter what she did, my mother loved me,' she said. 'She always loved me, but a minute of her love would have been enough.' Her eyes dismissed him.

'And what did you give me, you bitch,' he heard himself snarling, 'besides teeth marks?' She didn't answer, simply nudged him aside and crouched to tie the dogs back to the post. What she'd said to him made that soft achy part inside him curl up. What he'd said to her was making it petrify.

Yet even as he fumbled again with the bike chain, pulling at the dogs' leads which were getting in the way, he had to force himself to save what was left of his so-called pride, and stop himself from following her when she went back into the pub. What did she give him? She showed him how light changed on water. That would have been enough.

Nick stood outside the pub until the saloon doors stopped swinging. His helmet felt heavy, as if all the night's bitterness had been scooped into it. It was just another thing to crush his pride. He slipped the chinstrap over the handlebar and mounted the bicycle.

The doors flapped again as Robbie emerged with his arm slung around the Irish girl. 'No doubt about it – back to the bad old days, mate!' he yelled gleefully as Nick took off down the hill.

20

ON THE TWENTY-THIRD THEY CAME IN WITH A LITTLE electric saw, and Nick's armour was cut away. He flexed his fingers and twitched his bald white leg. For a moment he could only marvel at his hands, so light they almost levitated.

'The lad moves,' said Eric.

'You're young and you're strong, dear,' Beryl the physio said. 'Your wrists are in good order and you'll get your muscle back in no time.'

Eric sat on his perch, as if he were never going to fall off it, and nodded his head. Beryl rattled off her last instructions to Nick: 'Keep everything moving.'

Nurse Sunni took Nick's arm and guided him to the chair. He smelled her skin, a little salty under the Dettol, as she inspected the scab on his throat. 'That battle scar's just about healed,' she said. He winced. *Not quite.*

'What is it?'

'Nothing, just an ache.'

'You can wipe your own arse,' Eric hooted, 'so you're cured.'

'Really, Eric, you're getting so crude,' Nurse Sunni admonished.

Astonished at the sensation of bending his elbows, Nick scratched his cheek for the hell of it, sniffing at the odd, faint smell on his fingers; the whiff of old plaster lingered, but there was another scent, flighty, like something released. He took a deep slug of it.

Iris arrived with a gift for Nick, a new fat yellow ballpoint pen. 'Something to cheer you up. You should keep busy, jot down a few lyrics to keep you occupied.'

'Thanks, Iris.' The pen felt nicely weighty in his palm. But now that his hands were free to write, words were suddenly too raw, everything was still raw, and he regretted sending Jude those lyrics. 'I'll write something, for sure.'

Iris dug into her handbag again and brought out a coarse steel file. 'Are you sure you want to do this, love?'

'I promised.' He leaned over to kiss her ropy cheek before she turned to Eric, reminding him he was an old man and it would be another week before his plaster came off.

'Hardly worth bothering,' she murmured to Nick. 'We'll be back sooner or later, he's always breaking some bit of himself.' She looked up as Lindy made her entrance, bringing Trace for support. 'Hullo, Lindy love. Tracie, the shoemaker won't repair your slippers, so it's new ones, I'm afraid.' Iris shuffled over to Eric's bed and pulled out her magazines.

Lindy paled under her dark make-up as Nick flourished the nail file. That's not a file, that's a rasp,' she gasped.

Trace grabbed one of Nick's towels and draped it over his lap, ordering Lindy to sit down. Lindy sat, slid a foot from her stiletto and put it on his leg. Nick filed, and they all watched with fascinated horror as the towel began to fill with powdered heel-of-Lindy.

'How long will it last?' she asked when his hand wearied.

'Maybe a week if you tread lightly.'

'Gee, Lindy,' said Trace, 'your foot nearly fits into your shoe.'

When they'd gone, Nick picked up the notepad on which Iris had written his letter to Jude. Practically blushing at the corny words he was thinking of jotting down with his new fingers, he creased the edges of the pages gently, folding and unfolding, just because he could. He felt a pang, whether regret or relief, he didn't know. It could have been resolve. Some country songs, he reminded himself, are meant to be corny.

His legs were still wobbly, and he gingerly edged his way over to Eric, whose stare, now that Iris had left, once again reminded him of a cattle prod. 'Eric? Iris told me about Joe. I'm really sorry.'

Eric's eyes softened, which only made them look more bloodshot than usual. 'Thanks mate. Not a lot of time left for us, but we haven't given up on him.'

Nick went back to his chair. He picked up the pad again and began to write. *Dear Dave, you know that bloke sleeping in front of Beulah's . . .*

For once, he'd had had the good sense to keep his mouth shut. There were thousands of homeless men sleeping in doorways, but Iris would never forgive him if this one wasn't Joe. Dave Bear-claw didn't owe him a thing, but he'd do it, Nick was sure. Then he put the pen down. Somebody in town would always find out, Jude had said. *Trust the town*, he told himself. Yeah, but a little nudge won't hurt. He picked up the pen. The letter finished, he reached into his locker for the mini Mars bar that Lindy had left him and put it in his mouth all by himself. He let his head fall back. *Looks like chocolate, tastes like forgiveness.*

When he raised his head Maree was coming through the door. He had no idea what she'd say. If there was one thing he'd learnt since leaving home it was that people were breathtakingly, brilliantly, wondrously, inconsistent. He beamed at his mother. *Time to do some serious grovelling.*

21

Hey Nick,

The hospital said you'd survive, so I left. A lot of dust out here, and the pubs are hot and smoky and mostly empty, and it feels like home. I'm on my way back, going to see how Bruno's doing – might show him Leni's tree. It feels like I'm going to be fine. And the thing is, I still sing every song like it's my last. Thanks. Guess the lessons were for both of us.

Jude

P.S. Your song went down all right at the Targo pub – I don't want to be happy, I want to be with you, *seems to strike a chord with people around here. I'll play you the tune some day.*